A Pair of Deuces

A Pair of Deuces

JOHN REESE

DOUBLEDAY & COMPANY, INC.

GARDEN CITY, NEW YORK

1978

All of the characters in this book are fictitious,
and any resemblance to actual persons, living or
dead, is purely coincidental.

ISBN: 0-385-14007-X
Library of Congress Catalog Card Number 77-16852

For Ed and Gloria Guhl,
a pair of aces . . .

A Pair of Deuces

Chapter One

The big mare, nimbly pivoting on the end of her halter rope, lashed out with both hind feet at the young cowboy manipulating the long rope. The kid slid deftly aside, unafraid, and took a quick turn of the rope around the thick hitching post near the edge of the pole fence. With the mare on one side of it and he on the other, the cowboy began to take up slack.

"She's a fightin' fool," said Jim Pollock, who owned the mare and the whole Dot 4 Dot.

A whole side of beef was roasting in the coals of an open fire, in an iron rack Pollock had designed himself and had had built at the blacksmith shop in Kehoe Mesa. Jefferson Hewitt, perched on the top rail beside Pollock, had counted nearly a hundred men, women and children who had come for the Dot 4 Dot's annual fall whingding. It was probably the richest range in northern Arizona Territory, and Pollock could well afford this lavish hospitality. It was noon, and after the boys had had their fun with a bucking horse, everybody would eat.

"Yes," said Hewitt, "but that's no way to break a good horse, and she looks like a good one. What'll you take for her before they ruin her?"

"Jeff, I can't. They picked her out. She looked like the

meanest to ride, and we been doin' this for five years now."

"I hate to see a good horse spoiled."

Jim Pollock, a big, burly man who wore a gun as part of his clothing and got away with it even in the markets in Kansas City and Omaha, grunted. You give in a little to your neighbors, the grunt indicated, and you stay friends. If it cost you a good horse, that was part of your bargain with the fate that had made you a rich man.

The kid kept taking in slack until the mare's head was hard against the post. "Somebody get the saddle on her," he panted, "and then we'll see what luck we have bridling the damn ornery she-elephant."

She was a light brown mare, almost a bay, with black feet, mane and tail. She had come in off the rich Dot 4 Dot range in good shape, but a week in a dry corral had thinned her down until she looked rawboned and rough. Her eyes rolled redly. Her mouth hung with froth, and she was already sweat-soaked.

A dozen men leaped down from the fence and muscled the saddle on her back. With her head snubbed to the post, she was helpless. The halter had been made with thick tug-leather and the snap in the end of the rope would have held a ton.

"Git the bridle," said the kid who had roped her. His name was Dick Easton, and he had come here four years ago a ragged, rebellious, worthless runaway from some trashy family back East somewhere. Jim Pollock had taken him in and made a man and a top hand out of him, treating him like the son he had never had.

A man got down off the fence. "Hell with the bridle,"

he said, loudly. "Just git me a short halter rope and I'll show you how to ride her."

"The damn fool," Pollock muttered.

"Who is he?" Hewitt asked.

"Fella you're lookin' for. Frank Sanderson, and he's drunk enough to git himself killed. But I have to say that if anybody can ride her, he can."

"He's drunk!"

"About half. Frank's at his best that way."

Nobody was at his best half drunk, folklore to the contrary. Frank Sanderson was supposed to be good at anything, everything. Like Hewitt, he was a man of many talents, although they were different than Hewitt's. Excellent judge of livestock, good long-line driver of big teams, expert roper, almost a fast-draw artist with a .45. It took two or three good men to whip him, it was said, and they had better be big and strong and able to take punishment.

Frank Sanderson did not swagger, but there was a confident strut to his walk that was not an act. It had grown into him with the years, and it was one of the things that made strangers get out of his way. About forty, Hewitt judged, with cold blue eyes and a fair complexion mellowed like good shoe leather by the sun. Probably a little less than six feet and would scale a hundred and eighty in fighting flesh.

But shoulders like a draft horse, arms whose muscles rippled under the thin fabric of his old shirt, and hands like hams. With them he unbuckled his gun belt and handed it to the nearest man.

"Just git me a shank to snap to her halter," he said again. "Then let me git aboard and untie her."

"Frank," said Dick Easton, "you don't want to ride this mare without a tough bit in her mouth. I been takin' care of her for a week. They ain't no studhorse able to put up a stiffer fight."

Frank just narrowed his eyes and said nothing, to Hewitt a sure sign that he was drunker than he looked. Someone brought a six-foot, three-quarter-inch rope with a good snap in the end. The mare fought with her head as best she could, but in a few minutes the short rope was snapped to her halter ring along with the long lariat.

"Jim," Hewitt said, in a low voice, "the damn fool couldn't hit the ground with his hat in three throws. That mare will toss him and stomp him to death."

"Good riddance," Pollock whispered back. "I'm at the point where I just don't give a damn."

There were perhaps forty men perched on the top rail of the big corral. Not one but failed to see how drunk Sanderson was, Hewitt thought, yet they all made sure their feet were under them, ready to jump if the crazed, wild mare came their way.

Sanderson approached the mare like a professional bucking-horse rider—which in his time he had been. He grasped the saddle horn and nodded to the kid to turn her loose as he stepped up into the saddle. The way he mounted showed that, drunk or sober, he was powerful and sure-footed.

The kid unsnapped the long rope, gathered it in, and sprinted for the fence. He was on top of it and had thrown the lariat outside before the mare realized that she was free. Sanderson hauled at the short rope in his hand, twisting her head away from the snubbing post.

The mare literally exploded. She got her head down and her feet together and arched her back under the hated saddle. She went up in the air and came down hard, with all four feet bunched. She came crow-hopping across the corral toward where Hewitt and Pollock sat, and Jim Pollock threw one leg over the corral fence and prepared to drop to the ground outside.

Hewitt saw that Sanderson had lost his seat in the saddle the first time the horse hit the ground. Sanderson's changed expression told him that Sanderson knew it too. He was not afraid—not yet, anyway—merely surprised that it could happen.

On the fifth buck the horse crashed into the fence beneath Hewitt. Hewitt saw Sanderson lose his right stirrup and tilt to the left. His nose was already starting to bleed from the hard jolting he had taken. The halter rope slipped from his hand.

It was not conscious thought, but one of those idiot inspirations a man gets, that made Hewitt jump for the mare's head. He flung his arms around it some way and got hold of one of her ears. She threw up her head and her nose smashed into Hewitt's face. He opened his mouth and bit into her tender nose just above her upper lip.

He saw Sanderson hit the ground on his head, go over on his back, and lie still. The mare became motionless except for the tense quivering of her entire body. Her tender nose was the one place that made her vulnerable. The Indians had learned to tame a horse that way, and the white man had long known how to use the "twitch." This was a small loop of rope attached to a short stick of hardwood. Get the loop around a horse's upper lip and twist it tight with the stick, and you could hold the biggest, meanest studhorse in the world with one hand.

Behind him, Hewitt heard, "Git Frank out of there! Roll him onto a blanket because his back may be broke. And get a rope on that mare and snub her up again."

Hewitt took a step forward, forcing the mare backward. Another step, while he choked for breath. And still another. Dick Easton snapped the long rope to the halter ring and ran to the snubbing post to take a turn around it.

Hewitt let go and jumped back out of the way as Easton took a strain on the long rope. The mare began bucking again, but with each buck Easton took in more slack. In a moment he had her with her head tight against the post.

Hewitt did not see them rescue Sanderson, but he saw him lifted on a blanket over the gate with the top pole removed. There was no doctor here. Someone would have to do the doctor's job, and he knew who it would be.

"Jeff," Pollock shouted, "come look at this fella and tell us how bad he's hurt."

Only now was Hewitt realizing what he had done, the chance he had taken—all to save the life of a man he was trying to take to the gallows. He felt a tendency to tremble, but he thought he concealed it well as he climbed over the gate and knelt beside Sanderson.

The man was alive, that was certain. Hewitt put his ear to Sanderson's chest and heard a good, strong, steady heartbeat. He was limp as a rag and his color was bad, but there were no visible deformities to suggest broken bones.

"My guess," he said, "is that it's just a bad concussion, but we can't take any chances. Can we pick him up, blanket and all, and put him on a bed somewhere?"

Willing hands carried the unconscious man into the house where Edna, Jim Pollock's wife, led the way to one of the bedrooms in the big, sprawling log house. They lowered Sanderson on it gently and again Hewitt made what examination he could.

"Cold water is my best guess," he said. "Keep wiping his forehead and face down with cold water and see if he doesn't come to."

"Good thing he lit on his ivory haid," someone muttered. "Anyplace else would've killed the son-of-a-bitch."

⊙⊙⊙

The accident put only a brief pall on the fun of the barbecue. No one asked about Frank Sanderson's wife. She never went anywhere, and it would not occur to anyone to notify her that her husband was hurt. She was a good-looking woman, Hewitt had heard, faithful to a man who abused her shamefully, and practically a prisoner in her own home.

Some of the women took turns bathing Sanderson's forehead and face, but he did not move and, to Hewitt's mind, his breathing and heart action did not change. They dug the beef out of the bed of coals and began ladling out the beans and yams. There were no tables. Men and women separated into family groups and had their picnics on the ground.

There seemed to be no mourning for Sanderson, who did not have a friend on the place. The mare that had conquered him stood uncomfortably in the center of the corral, her head securely snubbed to the post. Edna Pollock had her duties between seeing that the food was served and the patient tended. Her husband and Jeff Hewitt ate together, standing a little apart.

"Jeff," said Pollock, "I sure got to hand it to you. You saved that worthless bastard's life." He shook his head admiringly. "I wouldn't even do that for you."

"I just didn't think," said Hewitt. "You see your chance and you take it."

"Not me!"

"Sure, I remember the time Sergeant Wicks was attacked by those four big Australians in San Francisco. You just stood there, didn't you."

Pollock grinned. "That was pure fun. A sojer's got to git it out of his system sometime. And as I recollect, you wasn't passin' the hat to take up the collection yourself."

Hewitt and Pollock had served in the same Army company a long, long time ago. Pollock had been a buck sergeant, Hewitt a corporal and the company clerk—only his name had not been Jefferson Hewitt then. They had gone through the episode together that had been recorded in Army records as a "serious disciplinary problem." Had it been officially called a mutiny—which it was—Pollock would have been one of the mutineers.

Hewitt, whose name then had been Hugh Goff, had left the Army after supplying the commanding general with the proof that attached responsibility to a half-drunk captain who was officer of the day, a green lieutenant who had merely done what the captain told him to do, and a weak, incompetent lieutenant-colonel who was unfit to command a company.

Afterward the general got him a job with the Pinkerton agency, at more money than he had ever dreamed of making, and he had left the comradeship of the military forever. He had not even thought of Jim Pollock until a couple of weeks ago, when he ran into him here.

Chapter Two

"Jim," he said, "what are you going to do with that horse?"

Pollock, his mouth full of rich, juicy beef, merely glanced at the mare in the center of the corral. "Try to peddle her, I reckon," he said. "She's a ruint horse as far as I'm concerned."

"No," said Hewitt, "she's not. She's teachable, if somebody gets on her with a bridle with a severe bit."

Pollock shook his head. "You can waste more time tryin' to break a horse that's throwed its man than it's worth."

"How much will you take for her? Get me a good, strong bridle with a curb chain and let me work her. I'll need a horse anyway."

"Not that one. She won't be fit for nothin'."

"How much do you want for her, damn it?"

Pollock grinned at him. "Same old Goff—I mean Hewitt. I just can't get used to your new name. All right, you kin have her for a ten spot, but I want you to do somethin' for me first. Write out where you want your mortal remains shipped so I don't have you on my hands along with that goddamn Frank Sanderson."

Hewitt took out his wad and peeled off a ten-dollar bill.

"You heard him," he said to a man standing nearby. "That's my horse now."

"Sure," said Pollock, pocketing the bill. "Give the boys another show." He raised his voice. "Hey, fellas, Jeff's goin' to bridle that mare and show us how to ride her."

"But all the rest of you except Dick Easton stay to hell back," Hewitt said. "Dick, find me a bridle with a curb chain and make sure it's a strong one."

The kid cowboy brought the bridle and helped Hewitt force the bit between the mare's teeth. They put it on over the halter and buckled it tightly, pulling the curb chain up as close as it could go. It would lock the horse's jaw in a painful grip by merely pulling on the reins. The Spaniards welded a spade-shaped piece of metal to the bit that could cut a horse's tongue to pieces. The American curb bit had merely a U-shaped curve in the bit to serve the same purpose without damaging the tongue.

Hewitt gathered the reins and stepped up into the saddle. The stirrups were a little long, and he had Easton adjust them before freeing the horse. "This is one of the reasons Sanderson hit the grit," he said. "I mean to have my feet under me."

"How about your hind end?" Easton asked.

"I don't know. Let's see. All right, turn her loose."

This time the mare knew instantly when she was free of the post. She tried to put her nose down between her knees to buck. Hewitt leaned back on the reins and she felt the curb chain take hold of her jaw, the curb bearing down on her tongue.

Up came her head. Up came her whole front end as she tried to throw herself backward to get rid of this man on her back. Hewitt snatched off his hat and leaned forward to slap it down over her head. "Hi! Hi! Hyo, you horse," he shouted.

Down came her front feet. Hewitt shouted for them to open the corral gate. The mare did her best. So did Hewitt. He had broken a few horses, but he had never claimed to be a bucking-horse rider. Keep her head up, keep her feet on the ground, and make her run it out—*if* he could.

She ran for the corral fence and tried to scrape him off. He hoisted one leg up to keep it from being crushed between horse and corral and slapped her over the side of the face with his hat again. She went sidling across the corral, every step a jolt that shook every bone in his body. He hauled her head around so that every sidewise step took her nearer to the open gate.

Suddenly she saw what she thought was freedom. She bunched her legs under her and jumped toward the gate, and Hewitt slapped her over the rump with his hat to keep her going. She went out of the corral at full speed, and Hewitt thought exultantly, Oh, but she's fast! And I'll bet she'll go forever . . .

She did her best to run out from under him and he let her run. Little by little he began to use the reins to steer her, to slow her, to make her go where he wanted her to go. The buildings of the Dot 4 Dot vanished, and so did the pine trees behind it.

Jim Pollock had built on the biggest, richest mesa he could find in the mountains of the northern end of the Territory. It snowed here in the winter and he had bear meat and venison whenever he wanted it, but he had had

to build several log bridges to give him access to Kehoe
Mesa and the road to Prescott.

They were in wild canyon country now, where the
mare could have taken a tumble down a slope that would
have killed them both. But by now, she was panting for
breath and responding—after a fashion—to the control of
the stern bit, and he was using it far more gently. Twice
he pulled her to a stop and let her rest. Twice, when he
slacked the reins and let her have her head, she thought
about bucking and changed her mind.

It was an hour before he turned her back toward the
Dot 4 Dot. She was a tired horse. He ran her hard and
then stopped her, and the moment she stopped he slid out
of the saddle. She rolled her eyes wildly at him but did
not fight him as he adjusted the bridle around her ears.
Nothing was wrong there, but it gave her something to
think about while she got used to him.

When he tried to mount her again, she shied out from
under him. He hauled back sharply on the reins and said,
"Cut that out!" She went up on her hind legs and he
hauled her down, and before she knew it he was in the
saddle again.

She just stood there. He leaned over and patted her
neck.

"Smart horse," he said, "smart horse! You and I are
going to get along together just fine."

He worked her hard, tiring her until the easy way out
was always her first thought. The big danger was that he
would get too attached to her, for in his business, he was
always going and coming, and attachments to horses and
people were both merely the groundwork for painful

partings. He dismounted, mounted, dismounted and mounted again and again.

A horse was not really smart. Everything was memory with a horse, and the "smart" one was one that could learn that certain actions inevitably brought certain reactions. Once they got it through their horse heads, nothing was ever going to get it out.

This country was riddled with hardrock gold claims gophered out of the canyon walls by brutal, hard work with pick, shovel, sledge hammer, star drill and dynamite. Some of them had made people fortunes before petering out; others had turned out to be just heartbreaking holes in the ground.

He made the mare go up to these dark holes and the "dumps" of excavated material beside each. He made her walk up and stand quietly beside an old, abandoned wreck of a wheelbarrow, not because he wanted to but because the mare did *not* want to.

It was two hours and a half, and the sun was well down in the west, before he rode her back to the Dot 4 Dot. Not a man, woman or child had left yet. "He'll be back," Jim Pollock had told them, "and I'll give two to one he's riding that mare when he arrives."

There were no takers. The mare was not yet fully "broken," and tomorrow she would object with every one of her aching muscles when he saddled and bridled her again. But she would remember. She would suddenly give up as though saying to herself, "Oh, well, what's the use? I can't get rid of this man anyway."

Dick Easton would have taken charge of her, but Hewitt shook his head. "Just bring me a currycomb and a brush," he said, "and stand by to help hold her." He removed the saddle himself and had Dick hold her by the bridle while he gave her her first taste of the comb and brush. She did not like the feeling of too much familiarity, but she found she itched all over after the afternoon's experience, and it seemed to her that this man meant well by her.

He peeled off the bridle and unsnapped the halter rope and let her loose in the corral with only the halter on. She went straight to the water tank that was fed by one of Jim Pollock's copious springs, and drank.

"Well," said Jim, "you've got yourself a horse, I'd say, Jeff."

"And a good one. How old is she?"

"Goin' on five, and never had a hand laid on her until we hazed her in here last week. What'll you take for her as she stands?"

"Money couldn't buy her now," Hewitt said. "Stay loose, though. You'll probably end up owning her."

"She's a sweetie!" Pollock said, enviously. "What you gonna call her?"

"That's as good a name as any. Sweetie."

"This is goin' to kill Frank Sanderson," a man in the crowd said. "If I's you, Mr. Hewitt, I wouldn't turn my back on him after this. You done rode the horse that whupped him and brought her back saddle-broke."

"How is he?"

"No change anybody can see." Pollock looked troubled. "Will you take another squint at him? I'd hate to have him lay there and die and his wife not even know it."

They went into the house. So far as Hewitt could tell

there had been no change. Sanderson still slept. He might be breathing a little harder, a sign of a bad concussion, but he doubted there was any skull fracture.

"One thing's sure, he's not going to be moved tonight," he said. "Shouldn't someone notify his wife?"

Silence a moment. Then Pollock blurted, "She's been left alone before plenty of times. He don't allow nobody at his cabin when he ain't there."

"Oh, the hell with that," Hewitt said. "I'll notify her if nobody else will. What's the matter, is the man crazy, or what?"

No one answered, but Pollock threw him a signal with a toss of his head and Hewitt followed him outside. The barbecue crowd was already breaking up, families starting back to their isolated farms and ranches and mineral claims after their one big celebration of the year. Now they could start looking forward to next year's community barbecue at the Dot 4 Dot.

"I'll get you a good horse," Pollock said. "My own, and I don't know nobody else I'd let ride him."

It was an excuse to go into the little roofed stable where Pollock's big, gray gelding had a box stall. Pollock got out the comb and brush and began cleaning him.

"I don't know this woman of Frank's worth a damn," he said, "and I don't know anybody else that does, either. She's stuck with him for four years, even when he was hanging around that Earp bunch trying to prove he was the toughest man in Tombstone. He's crazy about her, but he treats her like a dog, a damn dog!"

"In what way?"

"He's beat the hell out of her a few times for no reason

anybody could figure, once right in the middle of Prescott on a Saturday night."

"And people let him?"

"Jeff, he was set to draw his weapon, and nobody wants to go up against that kind of frolic."

"What's her name? Who is she?"

"Fella came through once and called her 'Charlie,' and said her maiden name was Law. Said she was the daughter of a Kansas homesteader and had run off with Frank. Said her name was Charlotte, but Frank overheard about then and beat the poor devil until he couldn't work for two weeks. Jest a kid, too."

"I see."

Pollock shouldered the saddle, then hesitated before throwing it on the gray. "Jeff," he said, "air you thinkin' Frank might be involved in that stage holdup?"

"Anybody could be involved in it, couldn't they? They got away clean with forty thousand dollars. The money has never turned up anywhere. We've found two dead men we think might have been involved in it. Our best guess is that three of them pulled the job and one of them killed the other two. Now you tell me how you find Number One without just looking people over."

"Frank could do it," Pollock said, in a low, thoughtful voice, "but I don't see how he could set on that much money and never spend a dime. Him and that poor wife of his'n work like dogs on that pitiful little old gold claim. If he had any part of forty thousand, he's got forty thousand places he could spend it."

"Not if he's smart enough and tough enough to forget

he's got it until the talk dies down," Hewitt said. "It always does, and nobody is interested except—"

"Except the private detectives that are paid to remember. I ain't going to say Frank *wouldn't* do it. I'm just going to say I know the son-of-a-bitch about as well as anybody, and I just can't see him waiting for a better time to spend all that money."

He saddled the horse, put the bridle on him, and led him out. "It'll be dark afore you git there," he said, "but she always leaves a lantern in a tree because sometimes Frank comes home so drunk he couldn't even see the mountain. And they got this big white dog that you'd have to kill before you could set foot on the place when she's there alone. Jeff, this ain't a job for a strange man."

"Nothing strange about me," Hewitt said, swinging up into the saddle of the gray. "She'll know I'm just about the plainest old cowboy in the world."

"Sure," said Pollock, "but will Frank?"

Chapter Three

Jim Pollock had some ordinary horses on the Dot 4 Dot but he was rapidly replacing them with the best. The gray, which he called Slocum after a captain he had admired in the Army, was one of the best. There was only one trail after you left the stage road. Jeff gave Slocum his head and let him take his time as he toiled up the slope toward Frank Sanderson's diggings.

He heard the hoarse barking of a big dog and a few minutes later glimpsed the twinkle of a lantern. He began whistling loudly, a sonorous old Methodist hymn, "Let Jesus Come into Your Heart."

The light went out and he knew that the woman, alarmed at the approach of a stranger, had blown it out and taken it into the cabin. Soon he could smell the thin reek of dynamite, that lasted for days after a big blast had been set off. He made a mental note that dynamite had cost somebody money. That meant that either (1) Frank Sanderson had made enough out of his diggings to buy some; (2) he had credit somewhere, an unlikely possibility considering his reputation; (3) he had savings no one knew about; or (4) he had access to other money no one knew about.

Not proof. Far from proof. Just something to keep in mind.

A big, short-haired, whitish dog came raging out of the shadowy outlines of the slant-roof cabin and barred their way. The gray horse pushed on until the dog stood his ground, barking furiously. When he stopped, Hewitt let him.

"Ma'am," he called, loudly, "Mrs. Sanderson, I'm staying at Jim Pollock's place, and your husband has been hurt and won't be home tonight."

No answer. He waited a moment.

"Mrs. Sanderson," he called in a louder voice, "your husband is in bad shape. I don't want to frighten you, but he's unconscious and may never regain consciousness. Don't you think you ought to be with him?"

He could not see her, but he knew she had opened the cabin door. "Don't come a foot closer," she said, "and stay on that horse or that dog will rip you to pieces. Now, who are you and what do you want? And I've got a double-barreled sixteen pointed at you."

"Mighty lean thanks for somebody who is trying to do you a favor," he said. "My name is Jeff Hewitt, and I'm an old friend of Jim Pollock's."

"How did Frank get hurt?"

"Trying to ride a bucking horse he shouldn't have boarded in the shape he was in. He was drunk, ma'am, and he's been out like a light for five or six hours by now."

Another silence. Then, "There's a lantern in the branch of that tree. Go over and light it and let me look at you. Who sent you here?"

"Jim Pollock. I've known him for fifteen years, Mrs.

Sanderson, and you've got a friend there whether you know it or not."

The dog continued to harass him and the gray as he rode under the big pine. He made out the outlines of the lantern, the globe still up, still warm, the wick still smoking. He got out a match and swiped it across the seat of his pants and touched it to the wick. He made sure that the light shone on his face and that he closed the lantern carefully so it would continue to shine on him.

"Honest to God, ma'am," he said, "I mean you no harm. They warned me not to come here when your husband is away, but he may die and I'm a stranger here, and I just haven't got sense enough to believe he'd resent it. A woman belongs with her husband when he's in the shape yours is in."

Silence.

He waited a minute and then said, "I'm going to get down now, and don't you worry about the dog. I get along fine with dogs. You tell me where you keep your horse and I'll get him ready while you get ready to go."

"I have no horse. Frank wouldn't want me there anyway."

"It doesn't matter much what a man wants if he's dying. I'm going to get down now—"

Slowly, carefully, he dismounted. The dog leaped at his face. Some people believed that Hewitt had a power over dogs. What he had was a knowledge of them, and one of the things he knew was that if you showed a dog you weren't afraid of him, half the battle was won. He gave the dog his forearm and let it worry it a moment painlessly before dropping back to growl in frustration.

"Sit!" he said, sharply, playing a hunch that anything Frank Sanderson owned would be thoroughly disciplined.

The dog sat. "Stay back!" the woman said, as he began walking toward the cabin in the dark.

"Now," he said, "that's no way to talk to a man who's only trying to be neighborly. If you've got no horse you're going to have to ride double, that's all. Fix up whatever you want to take along—"

"One more step and I pull the trigger," she said in a voice that betrayed her by trembling.

Instead of taking the step his left hand shot out and grabbed the shotgun, which was all he could see in the pitch-dark doorway. He played a hunch that she would not pull the trigger, and she did not. The gun came away from her grip easily.

He cried out a little as he saw her fall to the floor. He knelt beside her but could see nothing. The white dog came bounding back, ready to fight. He shot to his feet and cuffed it sharply over the side of the head with the back of his closed fist. The dog fell back but came on again. He slid on his glove and reached for its lower jaw, and missed.

He did not have to try again because the dog did it for him. He got his grip and hauled the dog down on his haunches. Now, he thought, what the hell do I do with it while I find out what's wrong with her . . .

The dog settled it by becoming docile. Hewitt brought the lantern and knelt beside the woman. She was dressed in bib overalls and a faded blouse. Her hair had been braided in two long braids and wound around her head and pinned there. Her face, when he turned her over, was ashen.

"Why," he said, "she's beautiful. And not much more than a kid!"

He carried the lantern into the cabin. There was a built-in bed in one corner, a little four-burner wood stove, a homemade table and two benches. And nothing else. He put the lantern on the table and picked the woman up and put her on the bed. She was so light that she had to be just skin and bones, and she did not move when he put her down.

He searched the cabin with the lantern. There was not a bite of food in the house, but there was a quart bottle of whiskey more than half full. He poured a little of it into a tin cup and added water from a pail with a gourd dipper.

He sat on the edge of the bed and raised her head, letting it rest on his arm. Immediately she seemed to become at least partly conscious again. She sipped the whiskey and water and gagged.

"Get it down you," he said, gently, "and try to keep it. Sometimes it's food, too."

She took another sip and suddenly pushed herself away from him. Her face looked wild in the dim lantern light, and more beautiful than ever.

"Who—who did you say you were?" she asked.

He told her again, slowly and in his gentlest voice. She shook her head.

"He'll kill me for leaving here," she said. "He'll kill you for coming after me. Please go away—please!"

"I'm going," he said, "but you're going with me. Where are your things?"

She began crying instead of answering. He took the lantern and ransacked the tiny cabin, thinking what an animal cage it was for a woman to live in. He found a few pieces of clothing—a relatively new dress, a petticoat, some drawers—and wrapped them in a bundle that he tied to the saddle horn. She struggled to her feet and stood watching him.

He paused in the doorway and put his hand on her shoulder. "How long since you have eaten anything?" he asked.

"A long time," she said slowly, dreamily. She repeated it incredulously, "So long! A long, long time."

"Is there no food in the house?"

"No."

"Then what has Frank eaten?"

She passed the back of her hand in bewilderment across her forehead. "I haven't seen him in a week."

"Then what have you been doing?"

"Trying to work the mine, like he said. He made a shot just before he left."

"Where was he going?"

"He said he had to see somebody and would be back the next day. What did you say your name was?"

"Jefferson Hewitt, ma'am."

"Then you're the one he wanted to see."

"Me? What for?"

"He said he was going to kill you."

"Kill me? For God's sake, why, ma'am?"

"I don't know."

She was light-headed from hunger and there was no use questioning her further. She did not resist as he led her to the horse. He swung her up in the saddle, and then helped her slide over to ride behind it. By the light of the lantern as he took one last look around he got a better look at her.

About thirty, he estimated, maybe younger. Big, brown, wide-set eyes and a wide mouth, tremulous now with fatigue, hunger and fear. The woman was numb, unable to think, unable to do anything except accept passively whatever happened.

There was no use closing the cabin door. He mounted and told her to put her arms around him, and started down the trail. The dog followed for a while, unnoticed by the woman, and then turned and loped back up the trail. He knew when the woman slept because her arms went slack and he had to haul the gray in and catch her before she fell.

Each time she whimpered a little, but said nothing. Reaching the level ground of the mesa and a familiar trail, the gray broke into an easy lope. In less than half a mile he saw riders coming toward him. He stopped the gray and dropped his hand to the butt of his .45, which he carried in a holster he had designed himself. It clipped to his belt so that the gun lay almost horizontal, held by a spring clip that gripped the front sight. One twist freed it, making it the fastest-drawing holster he knew.

"Who goes there?" he called.

"Jeff! It's us, we been getting worried about you," came Jim Pollock's voice.

He had come out with three of his most reliable men, including Dick Easton. The woman was conscious but not much more, and Pollock did not bother her. He rode beside Hewitt, alert to help her if she started to fall from the saddle.

He rode right up to the kitchen door and jumped down to take Mrs. Sanderson as she slid from the saddle. His wife held the door open. "Take her into our bedroom," she said. "Poor thing, she's white as a ghost."

"No," said Hewitt, "no bed. She's just starved, is all. Is there some milk or soup you can give her?"

They put her in a chair and let her lean her head in her arms on the table. Mrs. Pollock, a thin, strong, plain woman, held the mug while she drank milk greedily. She filled it again and put it on the table, and then turned to heat something on the stove.

"I can't get it through my head why I'm here," Mrs. Sanderson said. "Somebody told me that Frank was hurt, is that right?"

"Yes," said Mrs. Pollock, "but you quit worrying about him and take care of yourself. Do you like cold chicken? I've got lots of cold beef, but chicken is better when you're in your shape."

Hewitt and Pollock stepped outside, leaving the two women alone.

"How's Sanderson?" Hewitt asked.

"No change that I can see. I've got both of them here and one has got to go, and you can bet your bottom dollar it won't be that poor woman. Hell, she's starved half to death!"

"Jim," said Hewitt, "she was light-headed for a while, but she told me that Frank left her alone there about a week ago 'to see somebody.' Me. To kill me. Who knew I was around here?"

"Why, I never made no secret of it. It could get back to him, I reckon, without no trouble. Somebody that happened past his cabin."

"That happened past it—or that went there to tell him?"

Pollock was silent a moment. "Something to think about," he said, at length. "You know the best thing that could happen now? If the son-of-a-bitch never even came to! Because he's a bad one, Jeff. They say Wyatt Earp ducked a showdown with him seven or eight years ago. He claims that when he was a kid of fourteen, Wild Bill Hickock taught him how to shoot. That kind."

"A bad man. A real, honest-to-goodness gunnie. Everybody get out of my way."

"It ain't funny, Jeff."

"Jim, I've met lots of men like that. I knew both Wyatt and Morgan Earp at one time. I understand them and they understand me. Is there some other place you could take Mrs. Sanderson as soon as she's able to travel? You can't keep him from finding out she's here."

"What about him?"

"I mean to be at his bedside when he wakes up."

Chapter Four

Jefferson Hewitt—only his name had been Hugh Goff then—had come out of the Missouri Ozarks a near-illiterate boy who had to lie about his age to get into the Army. He had been an odd sort of recruit, quick to learn, quick to obey, and quick to catch the attention of his officers.

They never knew he was standoffish because he was ashamed of his ignorance. He set about educating himself by reading, by listening to the way his educated officers talked. He read everything he could lay his hands on and spent part of his second month's pay for a good dictionary. It was the only one at the Presidio of San Francisco, and he guarded it jealously.

He was not satisfied to learn just English. Hearing German recruits or Spanish-speaking men talk in their own language, and not being able to understand them, drove him crazy. He made friends with them, and with an Italian, too.

By the time he left the Army to work for the Pinkerton agency he was a fairly well-educated man. He spoke Spanish fluently, German almost as well, and could carry on a conversation in Italian or French. He was a man of many talents, and he developed them all as well as he could.

He had always been able to shoot, with either the long or the short gun. He saw to it that he remained a crack shot—and that his reputation exceeded his real ability. But his favorite weapon, when he could get close enough to use it, was a shot-filled sap of limp leather, and he was an artist with it.

He had a natural talent for drawing, and could have, he thought, been a real artist. He carried a set of professional portraitists' crayons and had carried on several investigative jobs while posing as an intinerant portrait artist.

He was an expert gambler and knew all the tricks of the cardsharps. He had paid an old tubercular cardsharp good money to teach him all he knew, and he could have made a living at the poker table. He knew within three or four hands when he was up against a crook.

He was an excellent livestock man and, in fact, had made his reputation with the Pinkertons working livestock cases. He was a good mechanic. From a doctor he sent up for murder he learned the nerves and muscles that were subject to spasm, and the little pressures and massage that relieved pain. The doctor, in turn, had learned them, he said, from a Chinese practitioner who had also gone up for murder.

He was a jack of all trades and master of none who had used half a dozen names and personalities in his work. He had chosen to *become* Jefferson Hewitt because Jefferson Hewitt's personality suited him best. Jefferson Hewitt was the man he would most like to be.

Years ago a Cheyenne bank had offered to back him and a German immigrant professor, Conrad Meuse, in a bonding company. Conrad was a bachelor about Hewitt's own age, a fussy dresser who liked polite society and high life. Conrad could not understand how Hewitt could go dirty and unshaven, sleeping in bed-buggy hotels or haylofts or on the ground. Above all, he could not understand how a man who lived that way on the job could build up such monstrous expense accounts.

They were both rich men. Conrad did the bonding of corporation and public officials from their office in Cheyenne. Hewitt did the field investigations—including the criminal cases that brought in more and more of their income. He was not sure how much money he had, because Conrad did the investing. He was a genius at money management, and the fees he earned investing other people's money went faithfully into the partnership pot.

Hewitt rarely got back to Cheyenne. He had no particular business there most of the time, and there was always a bothersome quarrel with Meuse about expenses when he did go there. They could not stand each other for very long at a time, but underneath they were very much alike—hardworking, avaricious, with tender spots of which both were half-ashamed.

They were the best of friends.

All night Hewitt sat in a room near Frank Sanderson's bed, going over what he knew about the case on which he was working. One of the things of which he had made a note was that Frank Sanderson used to be known as "Faro Frank" in Tombstone. He had cherished the nickname and the reputation there. But after the Tombstone days were behind him and he got married, he seemed to have made a brief effort to put all that behind him.

"Poker is my game," he said. "Give me five dollars and a clean deck, and I don't need a job."

For a while he had worked as a foreman on a ranch in New Mexico. There was talk that he had got into trouble there because some man tried to "get gay" with his bride.

He had turned up in Prescott about a year and a half ago, and got a job with a house builder. Shortly thereafter his wife turned up, and they lived in a small house near the edge of town. It was then and there that it became known that he was a drinking man. He rarely got drunk, yet no one ever saw him entirely sober, either.

He was a loner, a short-tempered, aggressive man who was a cinch to fail at a job working with a gang and end up prospecting for a mine. His wife had followed him faithfully, but she often remained out of people's sight, letting Frank buy the groceries—so often that word got around that she had to hide out until her bruises healed.

Lately they had been occasionally seen together, and when they were, Charlotte was a silent, nervous wraith who tagged after her husband like a child. Only once had she come into Kehoe Mesa to bring him home when he was too drunk to come home alone, and that was when they had run out of food at home. People heard him curse her then, but she helped him on his horse and he let her.

It was not, he reflected, an ideal marriage.

The North East Arizona Transport Company—called NEAT without humor by people who had to ride it, had been stuck up just a little over a year ago. Probably never before in its history had its strongbox carried so much hard cash. A combination of circumstances that would not happen once in ten years had put $40,000 in the strongbox and only one passenger in the coach.

The road had been barricaded with fallen trees where it skirted the edge of a canyon. Below it was a sheer drop of some four hundred feet—above it, a steep, brushy slope that could not hide a horse. The driver took a good look around before getting out, with his shotgun, to remove the wood piled in his way.

He was driving six mules, the leaders a pair of fine red ones worth five hundred dollars. The passenger, a Prescott businessman, got out to help the driver.

The first thing they heard was the *thud . . . thud . . .* of the lead mules dropping dead in their traces. Then came the crack of two rifles.

And then a masked man stood up in the brush not twenty feet above them, a six-gun in each hand. "Don't get no idees," he said, calmly, "because you ain't goin' noplace nohow. Just kindly step away from that shotgun and obey orders, and this is the worst that'll happen to you."

In a moment two other masked men came clambering down from the heights, carrying identical Winchester 73 rifles. It was they who had drilled the red mules neatly between the eyes. Until they got down to the road, the man with the two six-guns calmly stood his watch.

One of the riflemen jogged the driver in the abdomen with the muzzle of his gun. The strongbox on a NEAT coach was always chained and padlocked under the driver's seat, but the driver had to carry a key to put in and take out cargo.

"Let's have your key, you old turkey-faced fool," the man said.

"They took the key away from me this time," the driver said, tremulously.

The stick-up man merely jogged him again with the rifle, saying nothing.

"Honest to God, I swear that's true," the driver said. "I left the key at the last stop. Them was my orders. I wouldn't try to—"

The stick-up man merely elevated the rifle a little and shot him through the heart. He turned to the passenger. "How about you? I reckon you don't have no key," he said, wearily.

"I certainly do not. You're welcome to search me and my luggage," the passenger exclaimed.

"I know that. Well, get the hell out of the way and help unhook these other mules. We come prepared."

The other four mules were unharnessed and turned loose. The robbers brought out two sticks of dynamite, a primer and some fuse. The Prescott man was not an expert, but it seemed to him that they knew what they were doing. They advised him where to squat for safety when the blast went off. He knelt behind some boulders around a curve in the road about a hundred yards below, and ahead of, the stranded stage.

He heard the deafening blast, which reduced the coach to kindling. He heard the robbers talking, and without making out their words was satisfied that they had ruptured the chain and freed the company strongbox. They did not bother further with him. He heard them ride back up the road, but it was a long time before he came out of hiding.

The first person to come through on the road was a Deputy United States Marshal, Tom Coflin. At twenty-two, Tom was a little unsure of himself, but people respected him as a man and an officer. He always carried a notebook and a pencil, and he did a good job of taking notes of what was to be seen at the site of the murder and robbery.

And a good thing, because that evening a hard rain hit, and half the scrapwood that had been the coach had been washed down the slope. It was a week before trackers tracked down the other four mules.

Tom also had the Prescott businessman sit down and methodically try to write down everything he remembered about Suspects Numbers One, Two and Three, as he called them. Number One had a full brown beard—you could tell that by the way it bushed out the scarf he used as a mask. He stood about five-ten and was more than chunky, he was almost fat.

Number Two was an older man, with gray hair showing under his hat, and he wore boots that had once had fancy red leather piping around the tops. He was not as tall as he had been before he became bent and stooped, but he had big hands and was undoubtedly an expert with any gun he put in them.

Number Three had cut eye holes in a new, blue bandanna handkerchief. He had tucked it up under his hat and then tied it behind his head, so that no deductions could be drawn about his face. He never got close enough for the Prescott man to see his eyes. He was about of average height but to the Prescott man he looked powerful, quick on his feet.

Number One was the leader, no question about that. Number Two had been the one who popped up with two six-guns in his hands right after the mules were dropped.

Number One was found shot in the back of the neck, from long range, by a rifle slug that went all the way through him, up close to the Utah line. The Prescott man traveled all the way up there and was satisfied that this was the man. He had $1.85 in his pockets, and nothing else.

Number Two's body washed up in Micheltorena Creek, a few miles below Kehoe's Mesa. He still had on his red-piped boots, and again the Prescott man was sure this was one of the robbers. He had apparently been shot in the back, too. His pockets were empty.

The case had first come to Hewitt's attention because some of the stolen funds belonged to a bank whose officers were bonded by Bankers Bonding and Indemnity Company, the firm in which he and Conrad Meuse were partners. No question, their client was in the clear, and since he had lost only $1,800 he did not want to pay a big fee to track down the robbers.

But the New York company that was the real owner of North East Arizona Transport had finally put the case in Hewitt's hands.

Bring Number Three to justice, with proof, bring him in dead or alive, and the reward would be $2,000, plus expenses.

Bring back the $40,000 or any part of it, and the reward

would be 25 per cent of the amount recovered. No expenses.

The trail had gone cold, but by talking to people who had known Walt Keaton and Tom Duckworth (who had been Number Two), he came eventually back to Prescott. That was where Walt and Tom hung out. They came and went, came and went. But when you couldn't find them in Prescott, all you had to do was wait long enough and they would show up.

Hewitt began methodically searching around Prescott, first for the money the third bandit might be flinging about and, when that failed, for the kind of man who might have joined in the robbery and then murdered both his partners. The kind of man who could kill in cold blood, as Number Three had killed the stage driver.

From the next room came a low, whimpering sound of pain. It was almost four in the morning. Hewitt stepped out of his boots and picked up a candle and went into the room.

Frank Sanderson still lay, fully clothed, on the bed. He was stirring a little, as though he felt pain, but he was not awake. Hewitt went out with the candle and sat down in the next room.

Daylight came, and he dozed off sitting up. What awakened him was a weak, querulous cry from the next room:

"Hey! Hey! Where is everybody?"

A moment of silence, and then the creak of bedsprings.

"Oh God, I'm dizzy and my head's splittin'," Frank Sanderson moaned. "Where the hell am I? What happened, anyway?"

Chapter Five

The man was sitting up on the edge of the bed in his underwear, not very steadily, when Hewitt went in again with the candle. He was bleary of eye and of brain, but fighting with all his bull will to snatch understanding out of nowhere and close the gap between his last memory and this moment.

And this was the moment that Hewitt realized the kind of man he was up against. Not just a hard-drinking, bragging, fast-shooting bully who had known the Earp boys. Here was a brilliant mind gone crooked, a man of purpose whatever he did, and as cold-blooded a specimen as he had ever met.

"Who're you?" Sanderson demanded.

"Jeff Hewitt. I'm staying with the Pollocks and standing my watch taking care of you. You got dumped on your head off a bucking horse, don't you remember?" Hewitt answered.

"I got to go to the can."

"Don't try to stand up until I find the chamber pot!"

Sanderson muttered an obscenity and tried to stand up and fell back with a sharp cry of pain. From a sitting position he relaxed backward until he was resting on his elbows, his face still contorted with agony. In a moment he struggled up to where he was again sitting.

"Don't be a fool, man," Hewitt said, as gently as he could. "You're badly hurt, and you could kill yourself if you fell now." And a hell of a lot I'd care, he thought, if only I knew where the forty thousand is . . .

To have Hewitt help him and hold the chamber pot was the ultimate ignominy except one—to wet his pants. Hewitt found the pot in the commode and put it down beside the bed.

"Now, let's have hold of your arms and see if we can get you up on your feet, Mr. Sanderson," he said. "Then maybe I can get an arm around you and support you while you use the pot."

There was nothing else Sanderson could do, but the look on his face told Hewitt that this man would hate him for beholding this shamed moment of weakness as long as he lived. He took hold of Sanderson's powerful upper arms and lifted. Sanderson grasped Hewitt's arms and helped, and in a moment he was reeling dizzily on his sock feet. Gradually Hewitt slipped his left arm around him and discovered the man could stand. He leaned over to pick up the pot and held it while Sanderson used it copiously. He must have been suffering with the need to go, among other things.

Hewitt put the pot down and lowered Sanderson to the bed again. "Don't you remember?" he said. "The Pollock fall barbecue. You rode a brown mare without a bridle and she threw you."

"I lost a stirrup right in front of everybody," Sanderson said.

"Yep, and I know the sensation," Hewitt said, cheerfully. "You feel like a damn fool when it happens, but it happens to the best of us. Let me help you to lie down."

"I can help myself!"

Sanderson lowered himself to the bed, suppressing a moan. Hewitt carried the pot out, emptied it among the dead tomato vines, and rinsed it at the windmill. When he returned with it, Sanderson was still staring malevolently, like a trapped tiger only waiting to get loose.

"You're a Pinkerton," he said.

"I am not a Pinkerton," said Hewitt, "but I am a private detective. Jim Pollock and I were in the same company in the Army years ago. Now, what else do you want to know?"

In the flickering light of the candle, Sanderson's face changed, hardened. "Why are you after me?"

"I'm not after you."

"You're a goddamn liar," Sanderson said, softly. "You think I was in on that stage robbery, don't you?"

"Well, were you?" No answer. Hewitt went on, "There was a little matter of murder of the driver, too, and the murder of your two partners. Now that you've got the forty thousand dollars, what are you going to do with it? You can't go anywhere to spend it that the law can't catch up with you. Do you know the price on your head?"

Sanderson did not answer, but his eyes asked the question; so Hewitt went on, "Two thousand measly dollars, dead or alive! I've seen horse thieves with murder records worth more. The Tombstone days are over, *amigo*. You're just another two-bit backshooter who'll get it in the back yourself someday."

"No, I never will," Sanderson said, "because then you'd never find the money. And you never will, whether I'm alive or dead!"

"The hell I won't."

Sanderson closed his eyes a moment, fighting pain and vertigo. He opened them and managed a twisted, artificial smile.

"Mr. Detective," he said, "I'm the safest man in the world, you realize that? You're sitting there with a pair of deuces and flourishing your penny-ante wad like you was somebody, and I kin tell you to go screw and that's all you can do."

"That's right," Hewitt said, "deuces back to back. And they're good enough to beat the hell out of you because I've beaten better men with them. Get it through your marble head that your day is over. You lost yourself somewhere in Tombstone where you turned out to be just another second-rater. Hell, I knew Wyatt Earp! I heard the old poop talk for hours on end. He never once mentioned your name. You just didn't figure."

"Wait till I'm on my feet," Sanderson said. His meaning was clear: I'll kill you and you don't even dare shoot back, because where's the forty thousand gone then?

"That's the best thing for everybody, to get you on your feet," Hewitt said, heartily. "I'm a sort of half-baked doctor. At least I can locate damage to a body that untrained men would miss. Let's get you undressed and see just how badly hurt you are."

Sanderson did not object. He let Hewitt pull his pants off carefully, an inch at a time, and then his shirt. He wore only a pair of long, summerweight drawers, that looked as though they had never been washed since he bought them new.

Hewitt began probing the man's neck with sensitive fingers, bringing stifled moans of pain. He got up on the bed astride Sanderson, who lay on his stomach, and applied pressure all along the spine, sometimes with most of his own weight on his fingers. Nothing there.

He sat down on the edge of the bed and began feeling Sanderson's head, one small spot at a time with his fingertips. He knew how hard it was for Sanderson to choke down the groans of pain, but the man was tough.

"I think you lit squarely on top of your head on a small rock or something," Hewitt said, when he had finished. "You've got a localized concussion on the top of the brain and nothing will heal it but rest. You sprained your neck badly but there's nothing wrong with your spinal cord."

"How long?" Sanderson snarled.

"How long what?"

"Before I'm up and around."

"You'll be on your feet in a few days, able to feed yourself and go to the can. In a couple of weeks you may be able to ride a gentle horse, with luck. In a month you can buckle on your guns and play like you're a hell of a badman."

"Where the hell am I going to spend all that time in bed?"

"Right here. You never heard of Jim Pollock turning anybody out that needed help. Now go back to sleep, Mr. Sanderson, and quit worrying, because you didn't kill yourself even if you did give it a hell of a try."

He went out, taking the lamp and candle with him,

hearing the subdued grunts of pain and the rustle of bedding as Sanderson crawled under the blankets in just his drawers. He closed the door.

Someone was in the kitchen, trying to start a fire quietly in the big iron range. It was Edna Pollock, and she looked as though she had spent a long, sleepless night, too. Her eyes were red from weeping, and she could not help starting to cry again when she saw Hewitt.

"In a minute I'll have coffee," she said, "and Jim will be out for his breakfast."

She put the coffee on once she had a fire of pine knots roaring in the stove. Jim came in, carrying his shirt and yawning. It was like him to ask no questions when he saw his wife's grief-raddled face. Since he was a man who shaved daily, he turned his attention to honing his razor. His wife burst into talk as he stropped the blade.

"That poor girl!" she sobbed.

"How come?" her husband asked.

"Have you any idea how old she is? Nineteen! She won't be twenty until November."

Hewitt and Pollock exchanged looks, both thinking the same thing: *It's been a hell of a hard life for her, then, to look thirty today* . . .

"Does she know her husband is here?" Hewitt asked.

"No, and one or the other of them has got to be taken somewhere else before they find it out. So help me God, she's loyal to him! He beats her and starves her and treats her as he wouldn't treat a dog, yet she's loyal to him, and do you know why?"

Hewitt thought he knew. "He rescued her from the cribs somewhere, probably."

The woman nodded vigorously. "Fourteen years old and sold into a Wichita sporting house and kept full of opium until it was too late. They beat the hell out of her, too. I wish you could hear her tell it."

"Tell what?"

"How good Frank Sanderson looked when he came in and took one look at her and said, 'This girl is leavin' with me. Anybody care to object?' She's not very clear on what happened because she was so drugged, but some—some— I won't use the word *man*—"

"Try 'pimp,' then," Pollock suggested.

"All right, pimp," she said, her face flaming. "He started to reach for a gun, and she said it was just like lightning the way Frank got his out. He started beating the man over the face with the barrel of it and cut him to pieces."

"With the other girls looking on in terror," said Hewitt.

"Yes. Nobody dared oppose him."

"That would be his style. And then, off they rode into the sunset to be happy ever after."

Edna was crying openly now. "I knew such things happen, you can't help but know it, but I never knew a *good* girl—and she *is* a good girl—who'd been through it. He did treat her right for a while.

"He bought her clothes and a horse to ride, and took her on a vacation to Kansas City. He—he made love to her, but she says he was gentle and kind and *so* crazy about her! It was like heaven."

"Only then he ran out of money," Hewitt said.

Again she nodded and showered tears. "He tried to get her to—to make her—"

She could not say it. Hewitt and Pollock again looked at each other, and then Hewitt said, "He tried to pimp for her, and she wouldn't have any of it, right?"

"Yes. He tried it again in Dodge City and Coffeyville and Tulsa and Amarillo. And yet every time another man looked at her on the street in the nice clothes he had bought her, he took her back to the room and just beat the *hell* out of her."

Pollock finished shaving, put on his shirt, buttoned it and sat down to the table. "How about some breakfast, hon?" he said. "Nothing you tell us is strange to Jeff and me. First off, I reckon Jeff will join with me in saying that we mean for this little girl to have the chance she deserves."

"Amen," said Hewitt.

"She'll never leave him. She thinks she owes him her life. What a life!" said Edna.

"How about this?" Pollock said. "That little Proctor cabin is in good shape. Let her hide out up there. Tell her Frank is after her with a black-snake whip, and she has to give him time to sober up. Tell her the law is on Frank's tail, and she won't be seeing him for a while anyway—and when she does he'll be a son-of-a-bitch to get along with. I reckon she's hid out from him before."

"Yes, but the Proctor place is so far from anything, and how can a lone woman stay there by herself? I thought of that, too, only I couldn't stay with her and who else is there?"

"Jeff," said Pollock. "He's got work to do. He'll need a hidey and somebody to take care of it for him. The two of 'em can hide out there till doomsday. Just go talk to her.

Tell her Jeff will bring that goddamn vicious dog she's used to. Load her with some of that tincture of opium in the cabinet if you have to."

"I couldn't do that," said Mrs. Pollock.

"What do you want to do, hand her over to Frank right here in the house?"

Mrs. Pollock looked at Hewitt. "You'll take care of her? You—you won't take advantage of her?"

"Now that's a hell of a question to ask a friend of mine," said Pollock. "Do you think I'd say to do it if I was afeared he'd take her for himself?"

Chapter Six

Mrs. Pollock spent most of the day sewing things for Charlotte Sanderson. Jim had bought her a sewing machine only a few months ago, one of the modern pedal type, and she had already become expert on it. She "made over" some things and used some material she had bought because it was a bargain.

Jeff Hewitt got the brown mare out, while she was still stiff and sore from yesterday's session, and after a slight battle got her saddled and bridled. He made a point of riding her past Frank Sanderson's window a few times, making her behave, before setting out for a good training gallop on the road.

The more of the horse he saw, the better he liked her. He let her have one long, hard burst of runaway speed before gradually hauling her down. She fought the bit, fancying she had been about to go free, but he stopped her. She had barely worked up a sweat and was hardly panting at all.

He walked her a while to cool her out and then picked a flat stretch of road—not straight, but not pitted with chuckholes either—and gave her another run. This time she got the idea and stopped when he spoke to her and checked her in.

Oh lord, she was fast! She looked like an oversize bronco, but she had the chest, the barrel and legs of hot blood. Not Thoroughbred, not a Kentucky jumper. Probably a grandsire who had been a Standardbred coach horse, he judged.

Pollock was waiting when he returned, with the mare under easy control. "I seen you let her go, Jeff," he said. "She's a hell of a horse, ain't she?"

"Yes, and she's mine."

Jim made a face. "I been skinned in horse deals before, but never by a good friend. I'll remember this."

"You'll get her back. That's the hell of it with my job, Jim. I have no place to keep a horse and no way to get her there if I had. But you'll pay what she's worth, believe me."

"Listen, Jeff, we got a problem," Jim said. "Frank claims he's got the shakes and needs a drink."

"He probably does."

As though he had not heard, Jim went on, "He seen you riding that mare."

"I meant him to."

"First he asked if that was the horse that throwed him yesterday, and when I said it was, he called me a goddamn liar, right in my own home! I think that's why he got the shakes. Can't stand to think he can be beat at anything by anybody. But he swears he'll get out of here if he has to crawl, if I don't give him a drink."

"I'll give him one myself," Hewitt said. "You can come along and see how to handle the son-of-a-bitch, if you like."

In the kitchen he poured a six-ounce glass of good

hundred-proof whiskey. With Pollock following, he went to Sanderson's room. Frank had managed to pull on his pants, but his neck was too stiff to manage the shirt. He lay on his back with a pillow under his neck, his eyes glittering silent hatred.

But he managed to raise his head with a grimace, and then turn on one elbow, as they entered the room. "Hidy, Frank," Hewitt said, cheerfully. "Understand you've been seeing snakes."

"I said I had the shakes," Sanderson snarled. "I never said nothin' about seein' snakes."

"Sorry. My mistake. See if you can get part of this down, but watch yourself. It's bonded liquor, the kind you're not used to drinking, and it'll put hair on the *inside* of your chest."

Sanderson ignored the glass. "Where's a bottle? Damn a man who'll tantalize a man who's down flat on his back the way I am."

"This is all you get for now. A bottle won't make a badman out of you. This will make you feel better than you deserve to feel. Do you want it or don't you?"

Sanderson took the glass of whiskey and drained it. "Good stuff," he said, handing it back. "I seen you on that horse, Pinkerton."

"I am not a Pinkerton," said Hewitt, "but any horse you can't ride, let me know and I'll break her for you. Your trouble was the same trouble you've always had."

"How's that?"

"The horse had more sense than you had. Nobody your age, an old, broken-down has-been, has got any business trying to stay on a horse with just a halter."

Sanderson swore and tried to get out of bed, but dizziness and pain flattened him on the pillow again. He turned white and closed his eyes, but Hewitt stepped closer to the bed to goad him more.

"Just a little old pair of deuces back to back," he said, "but they've already got you looking at your hole card, haven't they?"

"Talk to a man like that when he's down and helpless," Sanderson gritted. "Wait till I get back on my feet, goddamn you."

Hewitt sat down on a chair, crossed his knees, and lighted a cigar. "Care for a smoke?"

"No!"

"They're two for a quarter, Frank. You never could afford a cigar this good unless you stole two bits from some shoe-shine boy."

No answer. Hewitt puffed rich cigar smoke and let Sanderson see him smile.

"You think I'm a cowardly bully, I reckon, Frank," he said. "Well, I'm bullying you for a purpose," Hewitt went on, when Sanderson only closed his eyes and refused to answer. "I want to see just what you will do when you get up on two legs and get a six-gun in your hands. I want to give you all the reason in the world to come after me, and then I'll outdraw you and kill you with one shot at any distance you choose."

He leaned closer. "And do you know why? You're a gunnie, a badman, an old Tombstone tough, and I never knew one of you that didn't have a yellow streak a mile wide. I've killed eight men, two with a long gun and six with this."

He opened his coat to show the .45 snuggled against his belly. Sanderson looked up at Pollock. "I got a gun somewhere, Jim," he said. "What did you do with it?"

"It's put away safe," Pollock said. "You kin have it back once you're on your feet and your brain is well."

"Nothing wrong with my brain."

"The hell there isn't," said Hewitt. "You're a coward, a sneak, a liar and a bully. You're a back-shooter and a wife-beater, and at the last moment you'll lose your nerve and try to get me from behind. And I'll still blow a hole through your chest that you could back a pair of oxen through."

"And lose forty thousand dollars," Sanderson said.

Hewitt smiled up at Jim Pollock. "You heard him say that, Jim. You know what forty thousand the cowardly hound means. No, Frank, I'll lay hands on the money before I let you come within range. That's called filling your hand. Three of a kind to go with my deuces, and where does that leave you?"

Again Sanderson looked up pleadingly at Jim Pollock. "Jim, are you goin' to let this fella set there and ride me in your own house? Can't you get me another stiff drink? How much do you expect of a man? I hurt all over, damn it!"

"Mr. Hewitt's the doctor, Frank," Pollock said.

"One more drink to help you sleep, Frank," said Hewitt, rising. "May all your dreams be pleasant ones."

Darkness fell, and Dick Easton began loading an old wagon with odd pieces of furniture. Pollock chose him because he was loyal, trustworthy, had guts and knew the easy way through the dark to the old Proctor cabin. The last thing to go in was a wooden box full of groceries, pots, pans and dishes.

Dick started off immediately, driving a pair of lively little horses that would be sure-footed on any road. The moment he was out of sight, Edna called them to supper.

The table, Hewitt noticed immediately, was set for four.

In a moment, Charlotte Sanderson came in. She still looked too thin, and haggard and drawn, but in her new dress and moccasins she was a different person. Edna had prepared her for what was plainly an ordeal. There was a touch of embarrassed shyness in the girl, and at the same time a slight belligerence that dared them to look down on her.

"You've met Mr. Hewitt, of course," said Edna, "but not my husband. This is Jim, Charlotte, and he's one of the richest men in Yavapai County and ready to spend every cent of it to make things come out right for you."

"Howdy." Jim dropped his arm across the girl's thin shoulders. "Don't reckon we're going to have much trouble, honey. Edna says you're good people, and that's what counts."

Hewitt pulled out a chair for her. She did not quite know what to do, but he nodded for her to take it and she did so with considerable natural grace. Edna put the meal on the table and sat down.

"I reckon," Jim said, "that this would be a good time to ask friend Jeff to return thanks. Me and Edna don't do it as often as we should, but havin' a nice girl like you at the table, now's the time."

She gave him a skeptical look but bowed her head when she saw the others bow theirs. "Lord," said Hewitt, "please bless this food and the hands that prepared it. Give of thy kindness and love and generous bounty to this girl who needs it, and to those who would help her. This we ask, knowing we can count on Thee to rescue the poor and friendless who only take the trouble to ask for help."

"I've never asked a soul for help," Charlotte said, when they had raised their heads and Edna was passing the dishes of food. "I've always stood on my own two feet."

"That's not quite true, Charlotte, and you know it," Hewitt said, with a smile. "But you tried, and that's what counts with the Lord and with us. Now we've got some news for you, but I better let Jim tell it."

Pollock cleared his throat. "I've got a nice little two-room cabin been empty so long there's not even a road to it. That's where you're going to hide out until this no-good Frank makes up his mind to leave you alone and let you live your own life."

"He never will," she said, "and I won't hide from him."

"Then he'll kill you, honey."

She shook her head. "He's threatened to but he never has yet."

"It's different this time. You know what he's runnin' from, don't you?"

"He's not running from anything."

"Then call it hiding from."

"It's too deep for me."

"The stage robbery and three murders, that's what," Pollock said. She merely stared at him, and he gave her a moment to digest that before going on, "Him and two others stuck up that stage and killed the driver in cold blood. They got away with forty thousand dollars, and then he shot down his two partners."

"No," she said, "no, that's not true."

"Where was he for about three weeks when that job was pulled?"

"Frank's often gone a long time. I'm used to being alone."

But she had turned white and stopped eating. Hewitt leaned over and patted her hand. "Charlotte," he said, "you know it as well as we do, and you've always known it, haven't you? And that's why he'll kill you, the same as he killed his partners. You owe him nothing, neither loyalty nor concealment."

"Where is he?" she said in a small, squeaky voice. "Where is he hiding now, do you know?"

"Right here, in the other end of this house, laid up in bed where he'll be for at least a week. The damn fool got drunk and rode the wrong horse yesterday. Now all he's got to do is lay there and swell up like a horned frog with hatred. Only you're going to be gone to my cabin and be hid out good long before that."

"No. I'm afraid to be alone now, anywhere. Let me go away somewhere. You're right, he'll kill me, he *did* rob that stage and—oh God, and he's right here in the house," she said, incoherently.

"You won't be alone, daughter," said Pollock. "Mr. Hewitt is going to be right there with you, and he'll go get your dog, too. And I guarantee this—I've knowed this feller since we was both young bucks in the Army, and if I say you're safe with him, you're safe."

Chapter Seven

It was a hard ride through canyons, up slopes and over rocky ridges in the dark, but Jim Pollock led the way confidently. Behind him, riding a fine gelding Jim had bought for Edna a few years ago, and wearing a short, split skirt that Edna had made for her, came Charlotte. One good thing if it came to a run for it, Hewitt thought— the girl could ride.

He brought up the rear on Sweetie, who had her own ideas about how to spend a pleasant night. She fought guidance continuously. When she could, she wanted to crowd Charlotte's horse and fight. Hewitt could only be glad Frank Sanderson could not see her misbehave.

They were almost there when they heard what sounded like Dick Easton, returning. They pulled off the rocky trail—it could hardly be called a road—and Jim put his fingers in his mouth and whistled a brief, piercing blast.

"H'yo!" came the answer.

Soon the kid came guiding his tired team down the dark trail and pulled up beside them. "I ain't sure how you'll want things arranged, Miz Sanderson," he said. "I put the bed up in the little back room and I th'owed Mr. Hewitt's straw tick in the corner of the kitchen."

"That's all right," Hewitt said. "I'll bunk somewhere out of doors, with the dog."

"What dog?"

"She has one. I'll go get him in the morning."

"Be cold sleepin' outside, this time of year. I'm like to freeze right now."

"Teach you not to go away at sundown with no warm jacket," Pollock said. "Go home and turn that team out in the big pasture, and make yourself skeerce in case Frank sees you."

They rode on. It was almost daylight before they came to the snug little cabin. It had begun life as a miner's hut, Pollock said, but the gold wasn't there and the feed was, so the builder had filed on a farm. "Made good money at it, too," he said, "and he built this cabin and then couldn't git a woman to live in it. So I bought the whole shebang from him at a fair price."

"Fair to whom?" Hewitt asked. Jim merely grunted, and Hewitt said, "This ten-dollar horse you sold me has got me aching in every joint."

"That's just cause you're gettin' old, Mr. Hewitt. I don't make deals. I just take people up on 'em when they're offered."

The front room had an iron stove like the one in Sanderson's cabin—like the ones in a thousand small cabins everywhere—but it was in better shape. There were a handsome, handmade table and four chairs bought from the store. There was a set of curtained shelves for groceries, pots and pans.

Heavy curtains covered the door between the two rooms. The bedroom was small, but it had two windows—

one large enough to serve as an emergency escape route. The thought of fire came to his mind. Frank Sanderson was capable of burning somebody out, even his own wife, and this place had been built of highly flammable pine logs.

They had brought two lanterns, one small lamp, two gallons of kerosene, and a supply of big candles. Pollock lighted one of the lanterns and hung it on a nail near the door between the two rooms.

"You're fixed up for everything but fresh meat," he said. "You're going to have to look for a fat Dot Four Dot calf and butcher it, Jeff."

"Don't worry about us."

"I do worry. You say Frank's a loner. It comes to me that maybe he *was*, maybe he'd *like* to be. But what if he got to where he *had* to take a pardner to pull this deal off?"

"We'll deal with that if it happens. I've thought of that, too."

The girl sat down in one of the chairs and folded her hands in her lap. "Hungry?" Pollock asked her.

She looked up at him with a tremulous smile, the first smile Hewitt had ever seen on her face. "Starved," she confessed. "It seems that all I've done is eat, and yet I'm so hungry I'm shaky."

"Then why don't we eat? Ma sent along a kittle of stew we could warm up, if Mr. Hewitt kin stoop to buildin' a fire. You just set there. I know where she put the stew and everything, and all we want to do tonight is fill up, anyway."

The stew was delicious. So was the loaf of fresh bread

Edna had sent along. But Hewitt worried about the glare
of fire and the shower of sparks that came out of the tall
stovepipe. He made a mental note that they would do all
their cooking by daylight, and Charlotte would just have
to put up with a cold cabin at night.

The two men lit another lantern and scouted the outside of the cabin while Charlotte washed the dishes. The
former owner had started to build a winter shelter for cattle with a shed roof. It had been extended only far
enough to shelter a couple of dozen critters, but it was
soundly built, and the roof was a vantage point from
which he could see everything.

"I'll bunk here," he decided. "I'll wake up and be down
before daylight, before anyone could spot me there."

They returned to the cabin so Pollock could say
good-by. Time to herself to do the dishes had been time to
think of her problems, and Charlotte was plainly not at
ease.

"I don't know," she said, "maybe I ought to go back
with you, Jim."

"Oh, shoot, you're livin' in a good cabin in the prettiest
place in Arizona!" Pollock replied. "You just go in there
and sleep and figger that, mebbe for the first time in your
life, you got somebody to shoulder part of your load."

She tried to smile, but tears glistened in her eyes. Pollock leaned over and gave her a light kiss on the forehead.
"You be happy, now!" he said. "See you in a day or two—
sooner if there's any reason."

He went outside and rode off in the darkness. The girl
faced Hewitt straightforwardly. "You don't have to bunk
outside, Mr. Hewitt," she said. "I trust you."

"I know you do," he said, smiling, "but I don't trust anybody who might come blundering around. Can you shoot a thirty-eight?"

"Yes, but I couldn't hit anything. They're too big for my hand."

"A thirty-two? I've got both."

"Oh yes, that would be better."

He wore a shoulder holster in which he carried the .38 when he could, the .32 when the other gun was too conspicuous there. He gave her the smaller gun and took note of how expertly she hefted it, tried its grip, hefted it again.

"You can shoot, can't you?" he said.

"Frank used to give me a gun like this one sometimes when fellas might get fresh, but he always took it away afterward. He taught me to shoot. He said I was pretty good."

"When *not* to shoot is sometimes the most important part of gunmanship."

"I know that," she said, soberly. Her face got a faraway and somewhat sad look.

"Ever have to shoot anyone?" he asked.

"Yes. A little old runty teamster in Santa Fe that made a dirty pest of himself."

"Wouldn't take 'no' for an answer, eh?"

She nodded. "They *told* him I was Frank's wife and to let me alone, but he kept pestering, and once he tried to corner me out on an empty lot where I was cutting greens for supper. I warned him and then I let him have it, right in the knee."

"You shot at his knee?" She nodded. "From how far away?" he went on.

"I reckon fifteen feet."

"That would qualify you for Marksman and some privileges in the Army."

"I told you, Frank said I was pretty good."

He nodded. "Now listen carefully. I'll be sleeping on the roof of the shed where I can see the front door but not your back window, the big one. You sleep with that gun under your pillow. If anybody tries to come through that window, don't warn him, don't waste time—just shoot to kill. Because one thing you can be sure of—he won't have any business there."

She nodded soberly. He took her into the house and showed her how to wire the front door securely shut. He did not ask her if she would be afraid. She would not be. Poor little tyke, everything that could happen to frighten her had already happened.

He took his bedroll and went to the unfinished shed. He stepped up into the fork of a tree and tossed the bedroll to the roof. He figured he had about an hour and a half to sleep. He jumped to the roof, rolled up in his blankets, and set his mind to awaken one and one-half hours later.

Manhunting forced a man to develop certain habits that often went against instinct. Hewitt had trained himself to sleep exactly as long as he wanted and awake refreshed. An hour and a half later he came awake, just as the light came to the canyon. He rolled up his bedroll, dropped to the ground with it—and then stopped in alarm as he heard a noise in the brush near the cabin.

He pulled the .45 out of his waist holster, shrank back against the shed and waited. A yearling heifer came out of the brush. Hard on her heels came an old cow, then another, and another.

He cocked the gun and waited. The heifer twice started to turn aside, but he held his fire. At about forty feet she turned to face him, sensing or scenting something wrong. He raised the gun and pressed the trigger gently.

The heifer dropped, and it pleased him to see that he had hit her between the eyes. He ran toward the cabin, shouting for the girl.

"It's only meat. I've killed a critter. Bring the butcher knife, Charlotte. We've got a hard day's work ahead of us."

She came barefoot out of the cabin, eyes full of sleep, the .32 in her hand. She saw the dead carcass less than a dozen feet from the door and it took a moment for her to grasp what had happened. Her look of terror changed to one of pleasure.

She ran back into the cabin. Edna Pollock had sent along only one butcher knife—not a very good one. It was sharp enough to stick the heifer and bleed her, but it badly needed honing. The girl picked the right rock—the one Hewitt himself would have chosen—and began sharpening it while he rigged a rope to swing the carcass up into a tree.

He found a stout piece of hickory for a gambrel, that most necessary of butcher's tools. He borrowed the knife to cut through the heifer's hind legs behind the main tendon. He thrust the ends of the gambrel under each tendon, and when he began to hoist her up head down, her hind legs were held wide apart and the strongest tendon in her body supported her weight.

He did not have to explain to the girl what he was doing. There seemed to be no homely, workaday chore that she had not done. She helped him skin out the carcass once the knife was sharp, and would have skinned out the head, too.

"Don't bother, Charlotte," he said. "We'll leave that for the wolves along with the hide. We've got more meat than we can eat here anyway."

Meat would freeze at night here, and be in no danger of quick spoilage by day at this time of year. But they did not need to be frugal. There would always be another beef handy to supply them with good, red meat. "We're not going to make good friends with Jim," he said, "shooting good heifer stock this way. Next time let's hope I get a crack at something less valuable."

"I like to get the stove good and hot and slice the liver thin and broil it right on top of the stove," she said. "Do you like that?"

"I surely do. I only wish we had some big slices of raw onion to go with it."

Her eyes shone. "Mrs. Pollock sent along a dozen onions. She says you can't keep house for a man without onions. We'll have a feast, Mr. Hewitt."

"Jeff," he corrected her.

"My friends generally call me Charlie," she replied, shyly.

"All right, Charlie, I'll list myself among them," he said.

It seemed to please her. He did not want to stir up ugly memories, but sometimes it was necessary.

"How many people have called you 'Charlie' in your lifetime, do you think?"

She frowned seriously. "Not Frank. He hated it. My stepbrother. He was the son-of-a-bitch that got me into that sporting house. A couple of the ladies in the house, they liked me and tried to take care of me, and they called me 'Charlie.' And when Frank was working in Tombstone—"

"What did he do there?"

"Bought and sold horses and cattle for a man, but there wasn't any money in it. The fellow he worked for, his wife was nice. She called me that."

Apparently she could think of no one else. It was a compliment to him and she did not realize it, but he did, and was grateful.

As they worked over the beef that day, he got her story out of her. It was not hard; she seemed to want to get it out of her system. Her stepfather had been foreman of an extra gang on the Santa Fe. He was a big, brutal, hard-drinking, hard-fighting, hard-swearing man. Her brow-beaten mother cooked for the gang and tried to bring up Charlie and her husband's worthless older son and daughter.

The daughter ran off with a man from the crew and nobody seemed to care. The boy, Charlie's stepbrother, was named Pat Herndon. At first he abused Charlie unmercifully. Shortly after his sister ran off, he changed, she said.

"He treated me real nice," she said. "I couldn't understand it when my mother said to watch out for him. He took me to a tent show once, and he used to pick sweet Williams on the prairie and bring them to me."

She was fourteen when he seduced her and talked her into running away to Wichita with him. They took rooms in what she thought was an ordinary rooming house. She never saw Pat Herndon again. "I didn't find out until a month later that Lottie Miller, the old bitch that ran the place, paid him a hundred dollars for me."

"How did Frank get you out?"

"He came up there one evening cold sober, and saw me and asked how the hell old I was. Lottie said twenty and he said, 'You're a goddamn lying bitch. I'm taking this girl out of here, and if you raise a hand to stop me, I'll mark you for life.'"

"And—?"

"Lottie wasn't giving up anything that cost her a hundred dollars without a fight. Frank gave it to her, and oh, it did me good to see it! He pistol-whipped her until I heard it took eighteen stitches to fix up her face. I guess it's cruel to feel good over that, but she made the porter and one of the girls hold me while she whipped my bare behind with a curtain rod. Believe me, after that you do what you're told."

She told it calmly, dispassionately, as though it had happened to someone else. Yet he could see, as she talked more and more slowly and dreamily, that she was beginning to awaken from what had been a nightmare she had never expected to end. Little by little her values were changing, all in one day.

"You understand, don't you," he said, "that you don't

owe Frank anything for taking you out of there. He hasn't done one unselfish thing in his life."

She nodded. "But he *did* get me out of there," she said, "and he never could get me to whore it in all the time I been with him."

"Charlie, there are times in life when we've got to make a flat-out decision based on one thing—is it right or wrong? Nothing he ever did was right. Don't you go wrong by misplaced loyalty. You've got to choose between Frank on the one hand, or Jim and Edna and me and a decent chance in life on the other. It's that simple."

"Oh, I know that," she said, calmly. "Edna and I talked about it. I never want to see Frank Sanderson again!"

"And if you do see him?"

She reached into her apron pocket and brought out the .32, then dropped it back in again. "And he knows I'd use it, too," she murmured.

Chapter Eight

Those eight days would always remain in Hewitt's memory as the happiest and most peaceful he had ever known. He was bone-weary, having worked a year and a half without a vacation. It was not the physical strain that wore him down, but the pressure of having to out-think, out-plan, and perhaps in the end out-shoot somebody. He would not have traded his demanding job for any job in the world, and yet every day of it took something out of him.

He slept lightly on the roof of the shed and spent his days working with Sweetie and scouting the country around the cabin until he knew every tree, every clump of brush, every rock that could hide a man. During the day the girl smoked thin slices of the tougher cuts of rump and shoulder over a slow fire outside, as Hewitt taught her. Meanwhile loin or ribs roasted in the Dutch oven Edna Pollock had loaned them, so that they ate meat sumptuously at night.

Each day Dick Easton came to visit them, bringing news as well as supplies—potatoes, beans, squash, flour and corn meal. Charlie had learned to cook as a child, and it was all coming back to her now.

But at sundown all lights went out, and they sat in the

cold, she with an old comforter wrapped around her, he with the collar of his sheepskin-lined coat turned up. Far to the south, in the desert, this was the hottest time of year, but each morning he woke up to see a half-inch of ice in the bucket with which he watered the horses.

He had no desire for the girl, while at the same time recognizing how desirable she was. It was like having a daughter, an untaught one who needed help. Her schooling had been hit-or-miss. She read well, everything she could get her hands on, and Dick Easton each day brought her magazines, dime novels and a few of Mrs. Pollock's books. She devoured them hungrily, a book or two a day.

She could write, but not well. She had learned to print so fast and clearly that she saw no need of learning script. He insisted on teaching her and had Dick bring paper and pencil. Like a child she rebelled at her lessons—like a stern schoolmaster he kept her at them, and made her proud of how quickly she developed a neat, legible script.

"Frank couldn't read writing, only printing," she said.

"There, you see why you need to write well," he said. "Anything he taught you, you could count on it—it's wrong."

It was amusing to watch Dick Easton fall in love, and see the girl look straight through him as though saying to herself, *I know what you want and you can just guess again.* Once Jim Pollock took Dick's place for the daily trip, and it was also amusing to see how disappointed she was.

Hewitt got Pollock aside and questioned him closely about Dick Easton. "A good boy," Jim said. "I'm going to make me a good manager out of that little hellion, although he don't know it yet. Someday I'll get old—I just don't see no way out of it, considerin' how hard it is to get out of bed some mornings. Well, that boy is going to be the son I never had if I have to skin his hind end with a belt buckle to learn him."

"How would you like to have a daughter-in-law, too?"

"I be dad-blamed!" Jim looked over to where Charlie was hanging out one of Hewitt's freshly washed shirts to dry. "So that's it!"

"That's what?"

"That's why Dick's so damn willing to make this miserable ride up here every day."

"That's it."

Jim leaned back and squinted. "When I picked me a wife, I went to church to get her. Good Presbyterian girl that knowed her Bible a hell of a lot better than she knowed what to do on our weddin' night. But she's a true, forgivin' Christian, and I think she'll be in favor of this. She worries about Dick and the trouble he could get into."

He scratched his back on the tree against which they were sitting. "Better put this off, though, until that bastard Frank Sanderson is dead," he said. "He'll kill any man that gets that girl. He's the kind of a single-minded rattlesnake that's going to strike even if he knows he'll be hit with a club when he does."

"How is he?"

"He don't seem to get no better. Just lays in there and stares at the ceilin'. Only gets up when Edna calls him to eat, or to go to the toilet. He asked me to get him something to make a cane with, and I got him a piece of second-growth white oak. He spends most of his time with a piece of glass, polishing it. Got himself a right nice-looking cane already."

"Watch him, Jim," Hewitt said, as a hint of alarm twitched through him. "He's faking it."

"I don't think so."

"I *know* so! He wasn't hurt that badly. Where do you keep his gun?"

"Hangin' on a nail just outside the kitchen, where Edna does her washin' and ironin'."

"He has seen it, I suppose."

"He'd be blind if he hadn't, but he ain't never made no move for it and he never mentions it."

"Jim, hide that gun! Hide every gun on the place. He's playing possum on you." Hewitt slammed his fist into his palm. "Damn it, I examined that man thoroughly. He could be out doing a day's work now."

"I can't make that judgment on a man I got in my own home, Jeff," Pollock said. "Either I kick him out in the shape he's in, and have it said I abused a man that got hurt on my own place and my own horse."

"What're you two looking so sad about?" Charlie called, as she went in the door of the cabin. "You look like you just found out the weasels got into your baby chicks."

She was in a gay mood today. From inside the house came the sound of a foolish little song she had remembered from childhood. She was a born actress with a clear, strong, true voice, and she sang because Hewitt had laughed heartily at her performance of the song:

Oh, a little dog was running 'round an engine,
And the engine, it was running through a fog.
   There came an awful yelp,
    Which the engine couldn't help—
'Cause the engine couldn't run around the dog!

"You want him to get his hands on her again?" Hewitt asked. "You want Dick Easton shot in the back? He's got a bad case on her, and Frank can smell that a mile off. You remember what she was when you first saw her! Look at her now. Want him to take her back?"

"I'll hide the guns," Pollock said, "and when Dick comes up tomorrow I'll send a rifle along with him, a Winchester seventy-three that cain't be beat."

"A forty-four-forty?"

"Onliest seventy-three model I know."

"Then look in that valise I left with you and you'll find some copper-jacketed ammunition for it. I've got a friend who is experimenting with smokeless powder, and I think he's got it this time. The others never had the hitting power, but this one has."

"Mind telling me who he is?"

"A self-educated explosives chemist with du Pont family. I met him in Washington some years ago, and he has asked me to try out a few things for him."

"You do get around," Pollock grunted, rising for the long, tiring ride back home. "By the way—seen any sign of Indians around here?"

"No sign of anybody. Jim, I'm just enjoying a vacation, the first real rest in years."

"I seen signs of four mounted ones, and they could be

'Paches. We ain't had no trouble with the 'Paches for years, but they play with their own decks. Don't know as I'd want one of 'em to see Charlie."

"I usually get along with Indians, but I'll remember."

Jim had barely left for home when the four Apaches came plodding their horses boldly up the canyon wall toward the cabin. None had saddles although all four used the white man's bridle. They were dark, squat, stony-faced men of indeterminate age, in ragged white man's clothing but with thick braids hanging out from under their wide hats.

Charlie was in the house, no protection at all if they meant business. He called to her in a low voice, "Stay out of it as long as you can but have that thirty-two handy." He had no coat on and his own .45 was in plain sight. He did not take it out.

Instead he picked up an ax and began splitting kindling as though he had not a care in the world. The four Indians rode up to where they could look past the house to the little corral where the two horses were kept. Either was worth all four of their horses.

"Hidy, men," Hewitt said, cheerfully. "Any of you speak English?"

"I do," said one of the younger ones, "but what you care? No business of yours."

"Hungry?"

"What you got to eat?"

"There's a beef roast and some potatoes about ready to come out. Light and tie and come in and eat with us."

"You got any whiskey?"

"Just enough for one drink around."

The young Indian spoke to the other three in their own tongue, in a low voice. Silently they dismounted, silently they tied their horses and stalked toward the cabin door.

Hewitt knew he might be making a bad mistake. But he also knew he might be making a worse one by antagonizing them. If they were looking for trouble, he and Charlie might be a match for them. The gun in her apron pocket would be a surprise that might make the difference.

One of them wore an old Colt Frontier .44 with the hammer no doubt resting on a live load. No trigger, which meant that it had been stolen from some gunnie, dead or alive, who fancied himself good enough to "fan" the gun instead of triggering it. The Indian might or might not be able to use it, but probably not well.

The others had the usual Apache knife, bought from some white renegade blacksmith and made from old files heated and hammered into shape and then ground down on an emery wheel. Their hard carbon steel made them the most dangerous knife in the world, in the right hands. And these would be the right hands.

The oldest of the Apaches went in first. He stopped at sight of Charlie, blocking the door and leaving Hewitt to wonder what the woman was doing.

"Come on in," he heard her say, serenely. "We're not fixed for company—not enough dishes—but I guess we can make out."

They herded through the door, belligerence and suspicion oozing from every pore in their sweaty bodies. The

six of them seemed to overflow the tiny room. Hewitt
clung to the thought, *I've got to have friends, and if I can
make friends of them, I don't need any others.*

Hewitt came in behind them and closed the door, to
show he had no fear of them. Charlie began hunting for
pans, anything that would serve for dishes. Hewitt offered
the Indians benches. They ignored him and stood there
impassively watching the girl. They even ignored the .45
that was in plain sight on his belly, a good sign.

"Do you want to cut this meat, Jeff, while I serve the
potatoes?" Charlie asked, without a tremor in her voice.
"I'd've put in more potatoes if I'd known we'd have company, but we'll just have to share."

Hewitt, now wet with nervous sweat, pushed through
the Indians to help her. She pointed to the butcher knife.
His heart gave an extra throb as he picked it up, and he
thought the Indians became a little more alert.

He tested the keen edge with his thumb and then
stropped it on the leg of his boot. He began carving the
meat, the last of the loin of the heifer plus a rib roast.
Charlie held the plates and pans while he put a generous
chunk of meat on each, and then she served the potatoes
that had been roasted with it.

The six plates and pans were full and arranged on the
table. Hewitt took the head of the table—one end, sitting
on an old nail keg. Charlie took some things off another
keg and sat at the other end. That left the two benches on
both sides of the table empty. He hoped they caught the
symbolism—that this was his home and he meant to be
master in it.

The oldest Apache suddenly made his move. He took

off his hat and straddled the bench and sat down, taking out his knife. The others followed his example, the one who spoke English sitting next to Charlie and on the same bench as the old man.

The old man stabbed the piece of meat on his plate and expertly snipped off a corner. He crammed it into the corner of his almost-toothless mouth and chewed a moment. He turned and muttered something to the young man.

"Grandfather say good meat," the youth translated. "Apache don't get much meat like this."

Hewitt ignored his fork and used the butcher knife to eat with. "Neither do we," he said. "We killed one of Jim Pollock's heifers, and this is prime. Enjoy it while we can because when this is gone, that's all there'll be. You know Jim Pollock?"

The old grandfather seemed to recognize the name. He spoke at length to the youth, who again translated, "Mr. Pollock good man. Mrs. Pollock good woman. Once Grandfather go their house, his thumb almost cut off. Mrs. Pollock sew it on, and see? Good as new, by God!"

He said something in Apache, and the old man proudly held up his scarred thumb. Thank God, Hewitt said to himself.

"How did he almost lose the thumb?" he asked. The old man would want to talk about it, he was sure.

The youth asked the question and then gave them the answer, "Goddamn funny how that happen. Grandfather get mad at fighting chicken that get whipped and try to cut his goddamn head off with a sharp ax. Old chicken, he gave a jump and Grandfather cut his thumb instead."

"How did you happen to go to Mrs. Pollock?"

"Where else?" The young Indian shrugged. "Anybody else kick his butt off the place. You know how it is with Apache in Arizona. We're Chemehuevi, live across the river in California. We don' mean no trouble, but who the hell gonna believe?"

"I know. An Apache is an Apache."

"An Apache is a som'bitch, what you mean, in Arizona."

Hewitt forced a good laugh. "Well, I'm from Missouri and Wyoming. If you're going to be sons-of-bitches, I guess I'll have to learn to change my ways."

"You treat Chemehuevi right, Chemehuevi treat you right."

"I've heard that," Hewitt said, although nothing he had heard in Arizona sounded remotely like that. An Apache was an Apache.

The four Indians swiftly cleaned up every bite of food. They ignored Charlie completely. The grandfather got up, picked his black hat up off the floor, and jammed it down over his head. He looked up and held up both hands, rolling his eyes to the ceiling to make a little speech. Again the youth had to translate,

"Grandfather still say the old prayers. Grandfather say 'thank you' for friend who give us to eat at their own table. And something else. You know a great, big bastard of a white man with long hair, smoke cigars, ride a paint horse? Slobber a little an' can't talk good."

"I can't place him." Hewitt looked at Charlie, who shook her head. He looked back at the Indian. "Why?"

"He been follerin' trail, tryin' fin' his way up here. I think we better kill him for you."

"No," said Hewitt, "don't do that. You'll just get yourselves in the worst kind of trouble, but thanks for the warning." He patted the .45 on his belly. "Now that we know about him, I think I can handle it."

"Ha!" The young Indian shook his head. "One gun? This feller him bad feller, b'lieve me!"

"How do you know?"

"We know, all right."

And they probably did. Hewitt took hold of the .45 and gave it the twist that freed it from its holster. "Come on. Let me show you something."

The Apaches followed him out of the door and Charlie came to the door to watch. They were facing to the West and the sun was in his eyes as it began its downward crescent, but that was just the way he wanted it because these born fighters would recognize the odds against him, too.

A harmless little chipmunk raced halfway across the yard some twenty feet away. It stopped to investigate something and then rose on its haunches for a look around.

Holding the gun in both hands to steady it, Hewitt squeezed the trigger. The chipmunk simply exploded as the big slug hit him. The Indians' expression did not change, but they said no more about killing the big man who was trying to find the cabin. The old man gave the young one orders.

"Grandfather say the creatures of the sky give you peace and safety. Only way I know how to say what he tell me."

"God be with us, you mean," said Charlie, suddenly.

The youth whirled and looked at her, surprised to hear sense in a woman. "Yeah," he said, "yeah, that's what he mean. God be with you."

Chapter Nine

The Indians went out of sight. He looked at Charlie and had a sudden foreboding that his brief idyll was over.

"You've got a hunch," he said.

"It could be Pat Herndon," she said. "He's got a lisp, and he slobbers. God, he's big! He was as big as his dad when he was fifteen, and he wanted to wear his hair long like Wild Bill Hickock."

"How could he know where you are?"

She shook her head. "I don't know. I didn't even know he was in the country. Frank said he heard he was down on the Brazos, running stolen cattle up from Mexico."

Hewitt nodded. "This would be a nice part of the country to take a vacation in if it got too hot for him down there. Any way he could have known Frank?"

"Oh, sure! They worked together in a mine just outside of Tombstone."

"Did Pat see you? Did he even know about you?"

Her lip curled. "Nobody knew about me. But you can't tell. He's a sneak. He'd love nothing better than to steal me back, Jeff. And I'd a lot rather go back to Frank. Pat, he—he's crazy."

"I wish I could lock them both in a cage, naked, and let them fight it out."

"Frank would kill him, Jeff. Pat—God, he's big! But Frank is big too, and he—he knows how to kill. With a gun. With a knife. With his bare hands. Pat would be just a big baby to him."

Hewitt made up his mind fast. He wished he had learned from the Apaches how close Herndon had come to the cabin, but transmitting that information probably had been more than they were able—or wanting—to do. They would warn him in return for his hospitality, but what business was it of theirs if the white men bushwhacked each other?

"I'm going to get some sleep," he said. "You get things cleaned up out here so you can stay inside, while I feed the horses. Tonight I'm going to walk sentry-go all night. I've got a bad hunch."

She laid a small hand lightly on his bare arm. "Jeff," she said, "if it's Pat, don't give him a chance! If he gets his hands on me, I swear I'll put a bullet through my own head."

She was terrified by old ghosts she had thought were left behind forever, more fearful of her stepbrother than of the man who called himself her husband. He slid an arm around her.

"Calm down, Charlie," he said, gruffly. "That's why I'm standing watch all night. You take the dog inside with you. I don't want him barking and giving me away if Herndon does come here."

The dog had not been at the cabin when they arrived, but he had turned up three days later, half starved and lonesome. Hewitt still could not handle him as well as the girl, and he thought Herndon would have his hands full, too, inside the small cabin.

He threw green branches to the horses and promised to stake them out to grass tomorrow. He brought the saddles and bridles into the house.

"Sleep on my bed for a few hours," Charlie begged, when he headed toward the door. "I don't want you out there asleep if he comes."

It made sense. He kicked off his boots and lay down on her bed. I'll give myself three hours, he decided. That'll bring it pretty close to sundown . . .

He ate a good meal and drank a whole pot of coffee. It went cold before he was through because they let the fire go out. It was odd how paralyzed the girl was by fear. Probably her seduction by Pat Herndon had something to do with it.

The West was hell on women and girls. A few like Edna Pollock got the breaks and were equal to the crises they faced. But it was chiefly a stag world to which women came for one purpose—to make money. Most of them ended up diseased, degraded and totally lost.

He had known one or two who had come West to work in the cribs, who had seen their mistake, and who got out one way or another. One opened her own sporting house and saloon. A few had married good men and made good wives. But there was a helpless quality about Charlie that meant she was as good as dead unless she got out of Arizona or came under some good man's protection. Her weakness was a deep, inborn decency which, after all her misfortunes, still survived. She could still believe the best of people, and God knew she had met the worst.

All night he prowled the dark outdoors. His ears tingled with cold, but he did not turn up the collar of his coat because he wanted to leave his hearing absolutely unimpaired. He kept his right hand inside his shirt, next to his belly, so it would be warm and limber if he had to go for his gun.

Nothing happened. Charlie slept until after daylight and then apologized for it. She turned the dog out and fried bacon and made biscuits for their breakfast. The dog seemed a little less suspicious of Hewitt this morning, and even took two or three pieces of biscuit from his hand.

"What's his name?" he asked.

"Frank just called him 'Dog' or 'White Dog.' I called him 'Whitey,' mostly."

"Where'd you get him?"

"Frank bought him from a teamster. He wanted to make sure nobody would come around me or the house."

"Well, we owe Frank that much, don't we?" he said.

Still nothing happened. He staked the two horses out on the thick grass that still had withstood the frost on the slope of the canyon that faced the west, as close to the house as he could tie them. It was one of the longest mornings of his life. It was when they were eating their midday dinner of beans that he made up his mind.

"Jim said he'd send Dick Easton up with a Winchester today," he said. "Dick won't know about Pat. You stay in the house with the dog and the thirty-two. I'm going to meet Dick."

"I wondered about that," she said. She was worried about him, but a man did whatever job he had to do and she had learned that if she had learned nothing else from the life she had led.

He combed and brushed Sweetie thoroughly, to get her used to being handled again. She resisted the saddle but he hauled her back sharply with the curb bit and made her stand while he laced it on. When he mounted she wanted to caper, but he disciplined her sternly and she quickly became docile.

"A smart horse," he said to Charlie, in the doorway. "She takes orders."

She got his meaning. She called Whitey, who wanted to follow Hewitt, and locked him inside the door with her. Hewitt started slowly down the wall of the canyon, holding Sweetie to a walk and listening intently.

Easton had made a habit of approaching the cabin from a different direction each time, so as not to wear a recognizable trail. It had been his own idea, and it was good thinking. Hewitt pushed Sweetie through some rough country to avoid any of the routes a man would ordinarily take, while keeping as close as he could to the main trail—such as it was.

He went so slowly that after two hours he was no more than a couple of miles from the house. They would be difficult miles for anybody, but the farther he went the more uneasy he became. He had learned long ago to play his hunches, at least when they bothered him as much as this one did.

We know a lot more than we think we know, Hewitt believed. He was sure that the mind absorbed a lot that never came to the surface as organized thought, and that when you played a deep hunch you were simply using knowledge you had but could not identify or put into words. One thing was sure—Charlie's deep unease about Pat Herndon was largely responsible for his feeling.

There would be no coincidence in it if Pat showed up here. Half of Tombstone, Tucson and Yuma eventually showed up in these cool mountains, usually to return to look blindly and stubbornly for gold when they got their strength back. And many a fugitive from the south had been picked up off the streets of Prescott or Kehoe Mesa by Deputy Marshal Tom Coflin.

"Usually," he had told Jim Pollock, "it shocks the hell out of them because I don't respect them for being wild and wooly badmen that ain't to be molested. But they learn fast."

He was going down a steep slope, leaning back in the saddle while Sweetie felt her way down the sliding dirt and shale. The horse spraddled to a stop, shooting her ears forward.

He heard it clearly, the echoing, crackling report of a forty-five. A man screamed distantly. The gun echoed again, the canyon wall catching the sound and throwing it back and forth until it died out.

And then, twice, the heavier boom of a rifle. That could mean Dick Easton. But the two forty-five shots and the scream might also mean that Dick had been hit and hurt before getting off his rifle shots.

No telling how far away it was. Hewitt dug in his spurs and crashed the horse through the brush to the best trail. He could not run her here, and in places a fast walk was impossible. He crossed a wide, shallow creek and saw where the four Apaches had forded it, and in deep dread only hoped to God that Dick had not been spooked into a fight with them.

The Apache trail vanished—you could count on that because hiding their trail was an old habit with them. Hewitt continued to push on down the steep slope, canyon walls towering on both sides, covered with trees and dense brush that could hide an army. He dared not tie the horse and leave her, even though he could probably make better time afoot.

That might be just making a present of a fine horse to some ambushing assassin. Neither could he turn her loose and leave himself afoot. He had to take his chances.

He heard bluejays and squirrels, he saw deer and one fat old bear, but not another sound came from whoever had done the shooting and the screaming. He tingled all over, expecting the thud of a slug in his body and then . . . black nothing.

He saw them suddenly where the creek doubled back ahead of him. Dick Easton was sitting on the ground, cuddling the rifle in his lap with his right hand and trying to stop the flow of blood from his left side with the other. He heard Hewitt coming, brought up the rifle painfully, and then recognized him.

Flat gravel left here by some long-ago flood floored this part of the canyon, and Sweetie did not have to be told it was time to run. Easton's tired horse had walked only a few feet away and stopped, but it began running when it saw Hewitt coming. He uncoiled his lariat, rode past Dick, and threw the best loop of his life.

It closed neatly around the runaway's head. The horse gave up and came back at the end of the rope. Hewitt slid out of the saddle, clinging to Sweetie's reins. She did not like the look of the man on the ground and fought coming closer.

Hewitt knelt. "Where'd he get you, Dick?" he asked.

"Side," said Easton. "Here."

Hewitt unbuckled the man's pants and pulled out his shirt-tail. The .45 slug had not left much of a hole where it went in, but there was a bloody mass of torn flesh where it emerged in front. Still, with care and luck, Dick Easton would ride again.

Hewitt told Easton to be quiet and save his strength. He used both their handkerchiefs to pack both wounds. Easton had lost some blood, not much but enough to frighten a man who had never seen a gunshot wound before, and the shock of a slug that big could be destructive. Consciousness was fading fast.

"Did you get a good look at him?" Hewitt asked.

Easton revived enough to say, "I heard him behind me and turned just as he let me have it. He fired again, but I was about to fall off'n my horse, and it missed. I got down and took a couple with the Winchester but he was already hellin' on down the canyon."

"Frank Sanderson?"

"Hell no! I was on the lookout for him."

"How come? Did he leave the Dot Four Dot?"

"Sometime between four this morning and six. No, this wasn't him."

"Can you describe him?"

"Don't have to. It was Pat Herndon."

"You know Herndon?"

It was too much for the kid. He had already passed out.

❦❦❦

Hewitt had to tie Sweetie while he got Easton back on his horse. Then came the problem of mounting the wild mare while still holding the wounded man in the saddle. He got a little help from Dick, who came to enough to grip the saddle horn with both hands. Hewitt wrenched the mare down with a hard haul on the stern curb bit.

He reached for Dick's reins. "Hang on, because this crazy mare isn't going to be any help. We'll get you to the cabin if you can just stay in the saddle."

A quarter of a mile up the trail, Dick started to topple to the ground. Hewitt slid off in time to catch him, but he almost lost control of the mare in doing it.

Four horsemen came crashing through the brush as hard as they could push their mounts. He let Dick slide to the ground and reached for his .45, but when he saw it was the Apaches, he could have wept with relief. He had a fractious horse, a wounded man and a long rifle to handle, and he needed as many hands as he could get.

"How about some help, boys?" he said. "I've got to get this man up to the cabin before he bleeds to death."

The old grandfather took his time dismounting and examining Dick's wound. He said something to the youth, who translated once more. "Old man say this not a man, this a girl-child if he die from this. I tell you, his horse is better than mine. I take his horse and you hand him up to me, how that?"

"And Pat is armed, unwounded and loose in the timber," Hewitt said.

Already Easton looked like a well man. He lay shirtless on Charlie's bed, compresses on both wounds and a wide bandage made from a petticoat around his middle. He looked slightly ashamed because of all the drama he had caused.

"I reckon so," he said, gloomily. "I should've knowed enough to be on the lookout for him when I seen him in town yesterday."

"How does it happen you know him, Dick?"

"Oh, shoot, he's been in and out of Prescott a dozen times that I know of. But listen, Mr. Hewitt, the hell of it is, he ain't no more trouble than a mosquito compared to Frank Sanderson."

"Tell me about that."

Charlie stood by the bedside silently as Dick told about it.

Yesterday, Jim had taken Sanderson's gun from the nail in the hall and locked it, with every other gun in the house, in the smokehouse where he cured his hams and bacon. It was built of four-inch timbers and locked with a heavy brass padlock, the only key to which he carried on his chain.

But it had not occurred to him to take the guns from his men. He had risen at four o'clock in the morning, hearing a sound in Sanderson's room. He went to the door and found Sanderson standing up and holding to the head of the bedstead.

"I'm so dizzy I don't know which way is up," Sanderson complained.

"Then set down," Jim said, curtly. "You got no business tryin' to stand up unless it's a case of have-to."

"But I got to go to the can."

"You can hold it until you're able to walk. I ain't carryin' no pot for you."

No use trying to go back to sleep. Pollock dressed and went out to take care of his horses. He did not pass Sanderson's room, had no idea that Sanderson had been shamming dizziness and had already left the house. In the cool, crisp morning, Jim Pollock felt cheerful, optimistic, full of energy.

Until, as he turned the corner of the woodshed, something crashed down on his head. His entire body buckled and down he went in a heap, unconscious.

Chapter Ten

Jim Pollock became conscious again as they were carrying him into the house. Edna, wrapped in a robe, was walking along beside him, holding his hand and weeping.

When consciousness came back, it came all at once, bringing strength with it. He had a splitting headache, but he knew he was not badly hurt. "Let me down," he said. "I'm all right. Go look for that son-of-a-bitch of a Sanderson, and shoot him in the back if you have to."

"Too late," one of the men replied. "He already helped himself to a gun and holster from the bunkhouse and your Buster horse. He's long gone and far away."

There were not even tracks to follow. Edna insisted that he lie down—or at least sit down. He ordered one of his men to get into Kehoe Mesa as fast as he could and get a wire off to Deputy Marshal Tom Coflin that Frank Sanderson had escaped and that the Dot 4 Dot was posting a one-thousand-dollar reward for him, dead or alive, on a charge of attempted murder.

The man found Jim's fine horse, Buster, ridden into the ground in Kehoe Mesa. A freight train bound for Prescott had come through at exactly the right moment. By the time the wire was received by Coflin, the train had arrived and Sanderson had vanished into thin air.

But an hour later, with four men tramping along after him, Sanderson had gone boldly into Sauzer's saloon and ordered breakfast. Sauzer knew two of the men. They were gun-heavy troublemakers he had ordered out of his saloon and told never to come back. But this did not seem to be exactly the time to make a point of it.

The five sat down at an empty poker table, facing the door. He served them ham and eggs and they said nothing about payment. Neither did he ask.

But someone must have seen them—someone must have run and stirred out Marshal Coflin. The batwing doors were flung open suddenly and the big, young, boyish-looking deputy marshal came in with his hand on his gun.

"Frank, goddamn it, you ought to know better than to show your face here," he said. "You're under arrest, so come along peaceable."

Without arising from his chair, Sanderson drew his gun and began firing. So did two of the men with him. As best Sauzer could recall, nine shots were fired. In any case, there were seven wounds in Coflin's young body. Any one of them would have killed him.

The gang got up and walked out calmly, reloading as they went, stepping over Coflin's body as though it were a piece of cordwood. People who heard the shots and came running were driven back by one shot from Sanderson's gun. It took a man's hat off without creasing his freshly combed hair.

They mounted five good horses and rode out of town, and nobody tried to stop them. The Territorial Governor had just appointed a sheriff for Yavapai County, Aubrey

Rush. He got there in a hurry, but he had not the slightest idea where to look for his men.

⬭⬭⬭

"Jim went to Kehoe Mesa and fired off a wire to Coflin," Easton said. "Aubrey answered it with a long-winded one telling everything that had took place. He even had the names of the four men with Frank."

"Was Pat Herndon one of them?"

"Hell no. Him and Frank would draw on sight! They hate each other's guts for some reason."

Hewitt looked at Charlie and saw her blink back tears of shame.

"Who were the four men?"

"They go by the handles of Slim Fraser, Cal Calvin, Jackie Heffernan and Joe Dunn. O'course, nobody knows if that's their real names. I knowed Slim and Jackie in Yuma, and I'd sooner shake hands with a rattlesnake. All four of 'em, Tom had ordered out of Prescott. I reckon if he'd knowed they was with Frank he'd've been carefuller about how he went in there."

Again Hewitt looked at Charlie. "Are any of those names familiar to you?"

"All of them," she squeaked. "Frank has had trouble with Slim Fraser, but they made it up. I haven't seen or heard of them in over a year."

"Reckon Frank had sent for them," Easton said, "and I wisht I knowed why."

Through the window, Hewitt saw the Apaches standing restlessly by their horses, tired of being ignored. He went out to take them a big pot of coffee and a tin cup.

You could be silent around an Indian and he respected it, he knew you were thinking about something. He took his turn with the coffee cup and helped drink the pot dry.

Frank Sanderson could not possibly have anticipated that he would be laid up and that Charlie would be stolen from him. Neither could he have got word to his four riffraff cronies since it happened. Obviously, he had some "job" in mind for them. Prescott was too hot to hold them after the murder of the deputy marshal, which had been deliberate.

Equally obvious, then, he was planning a robbery somewhere else. Kehoe Mesa seemed the logical place, and Jeff wished he could get word to Sheriff Rush about the hunch.

Kehoe Mesa had started as a small cattle spread, but its cowman owner had found gold and had taken some $200,000 out in a few years. He then sold his claim and moved East, while other miners riddled the slope with holes and drifts without finding gold. A small town had sprung up around the old ranch house. It was the coming of the railroad that had made the difference. The new owners of the Kehoe claim turned the town into a prosperous lumber mill and were cutting timber in five big camps nearby.

The Lumberman's Bank would be a good target for a crew of small-time badmen with a Tombstone background and big ideas. And if they tried that, it would bring the crew dangerously close to this cabin. A four-hours' ride straight across the mountains brought you to the railroad and thence to Kehoe Mesa.

Jeff made up his mind. "Could you fellows take care of

the woman for a few days?" he asked. "I've got to get her out of here. There's a gang of killers on the loose, and if they find her they'll steal or kill her—or worse. I wish I could get her off my hands until we wipe out this gang. I'll pay you well."

The young English-speaking man consulted with the others endlessly. "We ain't going home yet," he said. "We got a hidey, but it ain't no place for a woman, and we ain't got no women there."

"This is no place for a woman, either, and I'll trust you."

The old grandfather muttered something. "What if we take turns with her and then just ride away and leave what's left?"

Hewitt smiled. "You won't. She can stand a rough camp life, and she won't give you any trouble. You can keep in touch with me, and I'll tell you when to bring her back."

It was against the law for them to have left the reservation on the other side of the river, and keeping a white woman in camp would make it ten times worse. The idea appealed to them. If they had to make friends with one white man to make fools of the others, what was wrong with that?

He explained it to Charlie. She had been brought up to fear the irreconcilable, bloodthirsty Apache, but these had proved friendly so far and anything was better than facing Frank Sanderson or Pat Herndon. He took her by the arms and made her look at him.

"Jim and Edna told you I'd take care of you," he said, "and this doesn't look much like it, does it?"

She shook her head. "No, but I understand. I never expected to come out of this alive anyway."

"Believe me," he said, "you will. It'll be tough for a few days because I won't even know where you are. But if Pat Herndon gets the drop on me and cuts off a few fingers, one at a time, I can't tell him where you are, can I?"

She shivered. He went on, "Remember, they'll be more frightened of the 'Paches than you. These are good people, Charlie—different, but good. Now let's get you packed to go."

She took only a few clothes, a side of bacon—all they had, but the Indians loved it and thought it a noble gift of friendship—and her cup, plate and soup spoon. There was no drama in their departure. They simply rode off into the timber, the Apaches looking enviously at her fine horse. The old grandfather half-turned in the saddle to wave good-by—and they were gone.

Nothing was harder than planning when you had only a small percentage of the knowledge you needed, and he was so isolated here that he had no way of finding out what was happening until Jim Pollock sent word. He had a badly wounded man on his hands that he could not leave behind.

If Jeff Hewitt had ever needed patience, he needed it now.

⬤⬤⬤

At a quarter to three that afternoon, five men rode into Kehoe Mesa a few minutes apart. Four of them merely sat their horses inconspicuously, barely within sight of each other.

The fifth man, Frank Sanderson, walked stiffly into a small frame building on a stone foundation. Its single small window bore the legend:

LUMBERMAN'S NATIONAL BANK
C. J. Wells, Manager

The sore spot on the top of Sanderson's head had felt all right this morning, but now it was throbbing again. He felt a tendency to dizziness, and when he made certain quick movements a lightning-bolt of pain ran through his neck and made him want to weep. He was still in bad shape, but he dared not let the others know it. He knew how they would dispose of him and his disability.

An old man with glasses down on the end of his nose was at the narrow counter that served as a teller's department. There was no cage. He was rapidly counting the money in the till to balance his day's books preparatory to closing.

Sanderson went up and laid a fifty-dollar bill on the counter. "Wonder if you can bust that into tens and fives for me?" he said.

"Surely," said the teller.

Behind him, at a desk, sat C. J. Wells, who was responsible for this bank for the lumber company that owned it. Wells remembered that the James boys had often used this same approach to rob a bank. He leaned over to pick up the sawed-off, ten-gauge, double-barreled shotgun that leaned against the wall, ready to his left hand.

Frank Sanderson pulled the .45 he had stolen yesterday and, because it had a stiff trigger pull and was a strange gun to him, held it in both hands to shoot C. J. Wells through the head. He turned the gun to point it at the stunned cashier. He heard the horses of the other four clatter up outside.

"You want to get smart, too?" he asked the old cashier. "You want to be sensible and stay alive, or you want to get smart too?"

The old cashier turned to look as C. J. Wells toppled from his chair, half the back of his head blown off. "Oh, my stars!" he quavered.

Joe Dunn came into the bank and saw Frank Sanderson wince from a sudden, paralyzing pain in his neck and shoulders. He almost dropped the gun. Joe misunderstood.

He leaned across the counter and shot the old teller in the face. The impact knocked the old man backward over the body of C. J. Wells.

"You goddamned fool," said Frank. "Now who's going to open the vault?"

"Maybe it ain't locked," said Joe. "It's closing time, almost but not quite."

Frank, half mad with pain, said, "Almost but not quite! All right, try the handle but don't touch that goddamn combination!"

The others filed in. Cal Calvin waited at the door, according to plan, in case anyone tried to interfere. He had a .45 in his hand and a .38 in his hip pocket. The others went through the cash drawers and Wells's desk. Meanwhile Joe Dunn tugged helplessly at the brass lever on the big iron safe.

"It won't open," he said.

"Of course it won't open, you dumb son-of-a-bitch,"

Frank raged at him. "Get whatever there is, and let's get the hell out of here."

They took the time to rob the two bodies, finding three fifty-dollar bills and some change in Wells's pocket. They walked calmly outside. It was a small town, not more than a dozen business buildings outside the big sawmill a quarter of a mile away. There were a dozen houses and a big boarding house.

It was not time for a change of shifts yet, but the night shift was awake in the boarding house. Men heard the shots and came boiling out. The five took a few careful shots over their heads and then calmly rode out of town.

They trotted their nags until they had passed the sawmill. Here, despite his pain, Frank lashed his horse into a run. "Shut up!" he snarled when Joe Dunn kept trying to explain why he had shot the teller.

They came to a creek and walked their horses into it, but they did not ford it here. They splashed up the creek a hundred yards and then turned back in the direction of the town again. They skirted it back of the residences of the camp bosses and headed straight up the mountain into the wilderness.

Joe Dunn led the way because he knew this country better than anyone. There was a cabin up there that he knew about, deserted but in good shape, where they could hole up and rest their horses. They had food with them. The cabin was part of the Dot 4 Dot property, but nobody ever went there.

By dark, Frank was wondering if he was going to make it. He called a halt and made Joe tell them how to reach the cabin from here. You crossed this ridge, said Joe, and then the creek. On the other side you followed the creek until you saw heavy timber ahead of you. The cabin was in there close by. He was sure he could find it.

"If you can," said Frank, "so can we. Let's see how much we got."

They counted the loot, which came to $711.88. Even with his head pounding this way, Frank could figure fast. That came to about $142.37 each for a hard day's ride that hung two murders on them.

He pulled his gun and shot Joe Dunn in the back of the neck, severing both his spine and his jugular vein. Joe tumbled from his horse, killed instantly. Now the shares came to $177.97 each. He did not plan for them to remain that low for very long. The others could be spared as easy as Joe.

Chapter Eleven

Sheriff Aubrey Rush arrived at the cabin late the next afternoon with a posse of twelve, most of them drawn from the Dot 4 Dot. Jim Pollock was with them, and he immediately noticed Charlie's absence. Hewitt got him aside to explain it privately.

The minute Hewitt said "Apache," Jim held up his hand. "I don't want to know about it," he said. "Four male Apaches, including one kid, have been stealing everything they can lay hands on for two weeks. They'll be lucky if they don't get killed before they can get back to California."

"I think that's where they're heading," said Hewitt, "but they'll hole up somewhere until they can bring Charlotte back. And I'll get them a lawyer, whatever they need, if they do get caught."

"An Apache's promise ain't worth a damn."

"This one is, to me anyway."

"All right," said Pollock, "it'll be between you and me, but if there's an English-speaking kid among them, you're dealing with wanted men."

"Jim," said Hewitt, "haven't we got enough to do to round up Pat Herndon and Frank Sanderson and his gang without worrying about four Indians who are just robbing a few hen roosts and killing a few calves? It's a ritual pilgrimage to them, and they're about ready to go home and brag about it if I know Chemehuevis."

The posse had spread out to cover miles, meeting at the cabin. No one had seen any sign of the fugitives, but the sheriff had brought down a young deer and they could eat. While the posse rested and slept, Hewitt roasted venison. He fed them and sent them on their way again.

Sheriff Aubrey Rush was an old man with a bushy gray beard who had served three years as a deputy U. S. marshal. He bitterly resented the political upheaval that had cost him the job. "I don't want no part of it now," he said. "All I want is to bring these scalawags in to hang, and then I'll have me a peaceful county."

"And what you want is peace," Hewitt said.

"Right!"

"The hell you do," said Hewitt. "What you want is to *enforce* peace, and that's a different proposition. When Yavapai County is completely pacified, you let me know and I'll come be your office deputy."

"I can just imagine that," the old man said. But he was pleased nevertheless, as he led his men away.

Dick Easton was able to get around with almost no trouble. If he felt pain, he was too proud to admit it. Hewitt stationed him in the brush near the front of the house, where he could sit with the Winchester across his lap and guard the front from ambush. He had brought the shells loaded with the new smokeless powder.

"I got off a couple of shots, and they're really something!" he said. "She kicks like a mule so they must have hitting power, too."

"Wait and see."

Half an hour after the posse departed he heard Easton shout, "Just hold it right thar! Mr. Hewitt, come see what I catched."

It was the young, English-speaking Apache and he was carrying a dead man across the horse behind the saddle. Hewitt pacified Easton and waved the Indian on in. He unceremoniously dumped the body on the ground in front of the two men.

"You know this fella?" he asked.

The man had been shot in the back of the neck, obviously with a .45, the slug of which had gone on through. He was a stranger to Hewitt, a bony, rat-faced little man of no more than thirty-five, with bad teeth and a pimpled face.

"Sure," said Easton, "that's Joe Dunn. Frank has started to thin out his crew."

Hewitt looked at the Indian. "Could you find the place where you found him?"

The Indian grunted a yes.

"Could you track the people who left him there?"

"Sure, why not?"

"Will you go with me and help me run them down?"

"How much you pay me, dollar a day?"

"Is that what you want?"

"Yes."

"Then let's make it *two* dollars a day as long as you can show me we're on a trail. We'll start at daylight."

"Why not now? Long old ride."

"Suits me."

Easton pointed to Dunn's body. "You expect me to bury this garbage, the shape I'm in?"

"No, he'll keep several days in this weather. I'll put him up on top of the shed where he isn't quite so conspicuous, and we'll turn him over to Sheriff Rush."

He carried the dead body to the unfinished shed and hoisted him to the roof. He climbed up and straightened the body out on his back, with his hands crossed across his chest.

He felt only the same distant sort of pity that he felt for any born loser. Joe Dunn had been heading for just this ending since childhood, and nothing could have persuaded him that he was not having a hell of a time as a badman. But they all looked like this when they were dead, with nothing of nobility or even human qualities showing in their faces.

He saddled Sweetie, who did not want to be saddled, and followed the Indian. "We ought to know each other's names if we're going to ride together," Hewitt said. "I'm called Jeff."

"Me, Mac," said the Indian.

"Lead the way, Mac. You're in command."

They climbed constantly. There was no moon, but the Indian threaded his way through the timber as confidently as on a city street. Perhaps two hours passed. Then it was Hewitt who thought he saw a glimmer of light down in the bottom of the canyon toward their left.

He spoke softly to Mac, who turned just in time to see the light go out. The Indian scratched his head. "Wrong place," he said. "These other fellows, they're heading for Utah."

That would probably be Pat Herndon, who represented more unfinished business. "Tell you what, Mac," Hewitt said. "I want this fellow, too. Let's dismount and slip down the grade and wait for the daylight. If it's the wrong man, we've lost a few hours that we can make back."

"You payin' the two dollar a day. I don' care."

They walked their horses slowly down the canyon, the Indian in the lead. Hewitt could hear the impatient movements of a tied horse who could not get at all the feed he wanted, and just then Mac decided it was time to stop. They stood at their horses' heads, ready to shut off any sound they might make to signal the horse down below.

Hewitt had not realized how penetrating the autumn chill was until he had to stand as motionless as possible. He supposed it was at least three hours to daylight—endless hours of discomfort that could not be eased in any way. Mac seemed not to notice it, but he could not help but be suffering, too.

Several times they saw the fire flicker up through the brush, as the man down there put a few more small sticks on to keep himself warm without building a big blaze. They could see nothing of him, only his fire. He was probably taking a lot of pleasure out of that little fire, Hewitt thought, vengefully. Well, he would regret it, come daylight.

But before daylight came, they heard the man saddling and bridling his horse, swearing at it for its behavior. Either something had made him nervous or he just felt he had taken all the rest he could afford. In any case, it was the behavior of a fugitive, a man who had to make do with miniature comforts while better men slept peacefully under plenty of blankets in soft beds.

Without a word they began walking and leading their horses downward again. They stopped every moment or two, to listen.

He loomed up suddenly not a hundred feet in front of them—a big, hulking, round-shouldered man on foot, a good woodsman leading his horse. He did not see them. Hewitt had been keeping his gun-hand inside his shirt, warming it on his bare belly.

He took it out now and twisted the .45 out of its trick holster. He handed the reins of Sweetie to Mac and moved quickly to the left, to lessen the risk of stray bullets hitting the horses.

On came the man. Hewitt let him get within fifty feet.

"Hold it there, Herndon," he said, loudly and savagely. "I've got you covered."

"Jesus Christ!" the man said. He let go of his horse's reins and dived into the brush. Hewitt shot and heard the grunt of pain, but the man fired back, and the slug went screaming harmlessly high overhead.

It occurred to Hewitt that Herndon could not see them and had seriously misjudged the elevation. He spoke to Mac in a whisper.

"Wait here. I'm going to try to slip down there and take him alive."

"Easy for me," Mac whispered back.

"Just wait here and hold the horses."

Hewitt carried his shot-filled leather sap in his right hip pocket. Now he transferred it to his shirt pocket and shucked off his coat. He lay on his side, feet downward, and began hunching down toward where he had last seen Herndon dive into the brush. It was thick brush along here, and moving in silence meant moving a half inch at a time.

Nothing had ever seemed as black as this darkness. He listened, heard Herndon squirming and cursing under his breath. He gave up a little stealth then, counting on Herndon's own noise to conceal his.

He came at last to where he knew they were only a few feet apart. "Oh, lordie," Herndon was whispering, "oh, lordie, lordie, it hurts."

Hewitt got his legs under him and the sap in his hand. He hurtled over the brush, got a brief glimpse before he landed on his man, and had time to aim the snap of the sap. It caught Herndon squarely on the forehead, not hard enough to knock him out but hard enough to stun him.

Hewitt took the man's gun and threw it up toward Mac. "Pick up his gun and come give me a hand, and let's see what we've got here," he called.

The Apache tied the horses, found the gun, and came ambling down as though he had all day. He took a white man's match from his pocket and struck it on something and held it while they looked over their catch.

Hewitt's slug had caught Herndon in the foot, and he had been pulling his boot off. The foot was not mangled but it would be painful. Hewitt roughly pulled the other boot off.

"You're Pat Herndon?" he asked.

"What if I am?" Herndon mumbled groggily.

"That's all I wanted to know," Hewitt said. He stood up. "Catch his horse, and we'll take it and his boots and his gun with us. He's not going anywhere anyway."

"You can't leave a man here all shot up like this," Herndon mumbled, and he did slobber as he talked. "I'll bleed to death. This'll swell up and I'll get gangrene."

"A hell of a lot of pity you showed Charlotte," Hewitt replied, "but all right, I'll show you the difference between a human being and a rat like you. Mac, get a little fine wood here to build a fire and give me some light."

Herndon's boot was wrecked and his big foot had bled copiously. Hewitt knelt beside the lout and knew he had made a mistake when Herndon lunged for the .45 Hewitt wore on his belt. Hewitt had dropped the sap back in his shirt pocket.

He pulled it out and swung it in a short, vicious arc that hit Herndon's biceps when he had them taut. The big fellow's arm went limp, and he screamed a high, womanish scream of pain. Hewitt waggled the sap in front of his face, two inches from his nose.

"I can play with you with this all night if that's what you want," he said. "I'll leave every muscle in your body ruined for months. If you want to be fed with a spoon, just try that again."

"Oh God, my arm's broke!"

"Let's hope so, but I'm afraid not." Hewitt slapped Herndon sharply on the stomach. "Lie back and put your foot near the fire, so I can see it."

Bullets did strange things, could be deflected by trifles sometimes, or could smash through the heaviest substances. This one obviously had been deflected by Herndon's heavy boot so that it had merely skated across the top of the foot. Hewitt thought that the middle metatarsal bone, or whatever you called it, might be cracked, but he was certainly not crippled.

"Got a handkerchief?"

Herndon pulled two from his hip pocket. "One thing I can't stand is a dirty handkerchief," he said, "so that one is real clean."

"Yes, you're a nice, clean kid."

Herndon complained bitterly as Hewitt made a compress of the clean handkerchief and tied it on the foot with the dirty one. "Now," he said, "let's have that other boot."

"Oh, come on, you cain't—"

Hewitt snatched out the sap again and gave it a snap that was all wrist movement. He caught Herndon on the kneecap of the leg that had the good boot on it. Herndon screamed and lay still while Hewitt pulled off the boot.

Mac caught Herndon's horse. It was a good one, and it bore the Dot 4 Dot brand. Where the saddle and bridle had been stolen was anybody's guess. He let Mac lead the horse and keep the gun, but he got up into Sweetie's saddle holding both boots.

"A little back-shooting, a little horse stealing—you're already in bad shape, Herndon," he said. "I would love nothing better than to have you draw a gun on me sometime. If you're half smart, you'll lie there and wait until you're rescued."

"How long will that be?"

"I don't know," said Hewitt, "and I don't really care."

Chapter Twelve

All night he could only blunder along behind Mac. The Indian was not a communicative saddle pal. If he knew where he was going, he did not think it necessary to say where. All Hewitt could tell was that they were climbing steadily toward some kind of divide.

He tried to describe the four men they were after and tell why they were so desperately wanted by the law. If Mac understood, or if he cared one way or another, he did not bother to tell Hewitt.

Hewitt decided that Mac was taking his own route to intercept the fugitives, but that it was just a job to him. What the white men did to one another was no concern of his. Probably, too, Hewitt had earned his contempt by not killing Herndon. To have your enemy at your mercy, and then not merely let him live but help him dress his wound—what kind of foolishness was that?

Early daylight seeped in among the big trees, and they kept climbing. Suddenly Mac held up his hand, stopped his horse, and cocked his ear. Hewitt could hear it too, then, something coming through the brush somewhere ahead of them. It could be a cow, a buck deer, a bear.

Or it could be one of Frank Sanderson's mates. It sounded like a horse, one that was badly ridden by a tired

man. Mac and Hewitt dismounted and led their horses
into deep brush and waited at their horses' heads.

It was a seedy-looking old man on a big, raw-boned
bay horse, and both were in bad shape. The man's eyes
were closed and he was clinging to the saddle horn and
reeling in the saddle. The horse was limping badly from a
wound in his left hind leg that had bled all the way down
to his fetlock.

They waited until the rider was no more than a dozen
feet away. Hewitt took out his .45 and stepped out into
the open.

"You can stop right there," he said.

The man opened his eyes. "Oh God, oh God, oh God,"
he said, but his horse had already come to a stop. The
man's eyes closed and he tilted slowly out of the saddle, a
big .45 swinging on his hip.

Hewitt did not make the same mistake a second time.
He kept hold of his gun as he ran to put his shoulder up
and let the man's weight come down on it. He got his left
arm around him and lowered him to the ground. There
was no wound in front, but there was one that had bled a
little in his back, so he probably still had a slug in his
lungs.

The horse had been shot in the fleshy muscles of the
haunch, no doubt a long shot so that it, too, carried a slug.
And no doubt that it was done for. It would be a mercy to
kill it.

First Hewitt took the man's gun and handed it to Mac.
"Plenty gun, plenty cheap," the Apache said, shoving the
weapon into his pants pocket. Hewitt could hear water

running somewhere nearby, and there was a canteen on the wounded man's saddle.

"See if you can find the creek and fill that and bring it back, please, Mac," he said. "This fellow is in bad shape and I want him to talk."

Mac brought the icy water. Hewitt carefully trickled some of it into the man's mouth. He did not open his eyes, but in a moment he swallowed some of the water and then began to shake with a chill. He was having trouble breathing. Hewitt slid his left arm under him and half lifted him to a sitting position.

You saw men like this in Tombstone, or had a few years ago. You saw them on the Nueces and the Brazos, in camps along the Colorado or the Virgin, and if you caught them off-guard they ran like rabbits. Let them catch you off guard, and they'd kill you for your pocket knife.

These were the fabled badmen who were made celebrities by overblown prose written by commercial writers three thousand miles away. All of them had ridden with Frank and Jesse James, with the Cole brothers, the Youngers, the Daltons. All of them had notched their guns for the men they had killed as well as the ones they only wished they had. There were three notches carved in the walnut grips of the gun he had handed Mac.

They were not dangerous in a stand-up fight because they saw to it that they never got into one. They had never known the men they claimed to have known nor had they ever done an honest day's work if there was any alternative. A man like Frank Sanderson, who did have a

certain amount of wit, imagination and guts, could have
made them lick his boots.

The man's eyes opened and a little color came back to
his face. He looked up at Hewitt. "I's done for, ain't I?"
he said in a surprisingly strong voice.

"Probably," said Hewitt. "What hit you?"

"A forty-five. That goddamn Frank. I knowed he was
going to do it, and instead of shooting the son-of-a-bitch
in the back like I should, I just tried to run for it."

"And he took care of the horse first," said Hewitt, "and
when it stumbled, he planted one in you. What's your
name?"

"Cal Calvin," the man said with a certain pride. "I
reckon you've heered of me. Hell of a note, to die with a
bullet in my back after all the men I faced down."

"Sure, sure," said Hewitt. "Listen, you haven't got
long. Where is Frank headed? We'll take care of him if
you'll tell us that. Are the other two still with him?"

"They was when I left," said Calvin, "but they won't
be long if they don't just gun him down. That man is
crazy. He didn't have no call to shoot that banker, and he
just executed poor Joe. That was what it was, an execu-
tion. Just rode up behind him and shot him in the back of
the neck and said, 'There, that'll teach him not to f'ar
until he's told to!' Couldn't nobody open the safe, you see,
after Joe shot that feller."

"And now they split three ways instead of five," said
Hewitt.

Calvin did not notice how his voice was weakening as
he babbled on. He had a head for figures, that was clear.
The killing of Joe Dunn had raised the share of each by

$35.60, from $142.37 each to $177.97. If all three remain-
ing robbers survived, their shares would be increased by
$59.33 each, from $177.97 each to $237.29.

"Iffen he gits another one and him and the last one
splits even, it'll be three fifty-five, ninety-four each," said
Calvin, "but he won't. You always think you ain't going to
let nobody pull nothing like that on you, but I tell you—"

He began coughing, at first lightly and then harder and
harder. Suddenly the blood gushed from his mouth and
Hewitt quickly turned him over on his stomach to keep
him from strangling on it. But some major blood vessel
had given way, and he kept coughing and choking and
bleeding horribly until suddenly he went limp and was
dead.

The crippled horse was done for. Hewitt shot it between the eyes with more compassion than he had felt for
its rider. They rode on, leaving the dead man and dead
horse laying side by side. Up ahead, Mac began a sort of
soft, sing-song chant, no doubt a death-chant of some
kind, celebrating the end of an enemy.

He was following Cal Calvin's backtrack, and he was
the best tracker Hewitt had ever seen. Again and again
they crossed grassy parks that left no sign, but each time
Mac rode straight to where the horse had entered the
grass and picked up the sign in a creek bed or on bare
clay.

This was why the Army had hired Apache scouts in the
old days—and not so old at that. Hewitt could remember,
as a kid rookie at the Presidio, the talk of this 'Pache or
that one, hired as civilians, paid better than the enlisted
men and worth every cent of it. They had their privileges,

too, and even colonels commanding regiments treated them with deference.

The Apaches were so badly split, and there were so many separate families of them, that they might as well have been enemy tribes. You could hire a Chemehuevi to help you track Chiricahuas, and you could hire a fierce Chiricahua to track Chemehuevis. That made him a traitor to his people, a worse enemy than the soldiers, and it was sure death if one of them was caught by his own relatives.

Therefore, they were single-minded, silent, uncommunicative outlaws living a day-to-day truce for the white man's rations, without respecting him any more than they ever had. Every payday they got drunk, but they made sure they did it in camp, something no enlisted man would dare to do.

They were nearing the summit of the divide when Mac suddenly stopped. He dismounted and signaled for Hewitt to do the same thing.

"Why?" Hewitt asked, as he got down.

Mac pointed to the tracks in the dusty slope.

"Him limp," he said. "Him bad shape, not go very far. We better walk."

They walked, leading their horses, for no more than a steep half mile. They saw a bony sorrel horse standing hipshot in the sunlight, reins trailing on the ground. It raised its head but did not try to get away as they approached.

Not a dozen feet away lay the body of a dead man. He had been shot twice, once in the right upper arm and once in the head, just above the right ear. You could almost see it happening—Frank riding up beside him and taking his first quick shot into the man's gun arm and then blasting him in the head.

And then riding on. Now he and the last man were worth $355.94 each, by Hewitt's computation. He got down and examined the dead man. He had no papers in his pockets at all. He was probably in his late thirties, but bad food and bad whiskey had aged him prematurely.

His left inner arm was decorated with a big tattoo that he had probably got in some San Francisco Chinatown joint. There was a winged dragon, breathing fire, perched on a stump. Above it fluttered a blue dove carrying a flower in its beak.

On the stump were the initials, J.H. Here, then, in the Arizona highlands above the winter snow line, Jackie Heffernan had died by his own partner's gun. Net profit to each of the two remaining men, $118.65, give or take a penny or two.

He examined the horse carefully. It was not wounded, just worn out. It had a big, flowing, Mexican brand, and probably had been ridden hard all the way up from below the border. It had a chance here, if a mountain lion did not attack it before it rested and ate and got in shape again.

He unsaddled and unbridled it and gave it a friendly slap on the rump. The sorrel took it as a release from duty to the dead man and went limping up to where the grass grew. Retail crime for $711.88 in loot was hell on partners and horses, but maybe this one could survive.

❈❈❈

Late in the afternoon, when they were gaunt with hunger and so full of water that Hewitt felt he sloshed with every step of his horse, they heard men shouting far behind them. No outlaw would make a fool of himself with that kind of noise. Sheriff Aubrey Rush's posse had picked up the trail, and one of them probably had discovered Jackie Heffernan's body.

The Lumberman's National Bank was, beyond all doubt, bonded by Bankers Bonding and Indemnity Company for the good behavior of its officers. BB&I would not be liable for a loss here, but it was policy to take an interest in robberies and post rewards. Conrad Meuse would already have been advised of the murder of C. J. Wells and his clerk, and would have offered a reward. And, no doubt, he now was burning up the wires, trying to reach Hewitt to warn him to collect the reward himself before they had to pay it out to someone else.

The posse, for instance. Hewitt would cheerfully pay every member a bonus of one hundred dollars because that was the way a company made friends. But it would be unforgivable extravagance to let Aubrey Rush and his men share the reward—probably $2,000—that Conrad would offer.

This was, after all, a business with Hewitt, not a hobby. "Come on, Mac," he said. "Let's ride like hell."

Chapter Thirteen

You had to put yourself in the other fellow's place, in this case two other fellows, since Frank Sanderson still had Slim Fraser on his hands. They would both be scared stiff and pushing to make distance, yet neither would have any idea how close pursuit still was.

You could count on Slim Fraser being a little uneasy about now. Frank already had a reputation of disposing of his crime partners, and Slim being just a little uneasy to begin with, might be getting downright scared after what had happened to Joe Dunn, Cal Calvin, and Jackie Heffernan.

He'd be watching Frank like a hawk, and Frank would be sweet-talking him for all he was worth. Frank was not in good shape himself, and the tables might not be hard to turn. It could be his body left to stiffen on the trail while Slim rode off with the whole $711.88.

"I knowed I could count on you," Frank would be saying, "and I was right. You and me done everything right. But them other three fools—a man's a fool to depend on them! That Joe, shooting the one man that could open the safe for us, and then Cal and Jackie tryin' to run off like the dirty double-crossing cowards they was."

"Sure," Slim would gulp, "sure."

"You and me, we're going to make a team," Frank would say. "Find us a fat country bank and bust it ourselves. Waltz out of there with three, four thousand apiece. But we got to lay low for a spell. We barely got walkin'-around money now."

And Frank would have it in his pocket, all $711.88 of it. You could count on that.

Also, you could count on it that the moment Slim gave him a chance, Frank would cut down on him. Gun him down like he would a mad dog. Take the best of the two horses and, unencumbered by partners and their own plans, be that much harder to catch.

"Mac," Hewitt said. "I'm going to fire a couple, just to let them know we're behind them."

Mac scowled. "Why?"

"There's a fair chance," Hewitt said, "that Slim Fraser is on our side. That he's hoping something, anything, will happen to keep Frank from killing him as he did the other three. I want them to hear shots because Frank will know we'll hear if he fires. Maybe that will cramp his style a little."

The Indian nodded. Hewitt aimed his .45 into the air and fired. He waited a couple of seconds and fired again. As he rode he reloaded.

A few moments later, Mac drew his own gun, pointed it skyward, and looked back with a question on his face. "Good idea," Hewitt said, nodding. "Let them surmise it's a party, signaling."

Mac fired twice and reloaded. They stepped up the pace of their horses despite the stiffness of the climb, Mac leaning down to watch for signs. Both listened carefully for gunfire up ahead.

They heard nothing. As they neared the summit the country grew rockier and rougher, and the trails narrower. Up ahead, somebody's horse was getting tired, to judge by the way his hind feet had slipped here and there. Somebody could go over the edge easily if those missteps continued.

An hour passed. Two hours. Now they were up above the elevations at which the big trees grew. There were only scrub pines and some brush here, and anyone with the nerve—or the desperation—could leave their horses tied somewhere, walk back, and squat behind any of a hundred points of cover.

This was a chance you took when you crowded a man too close. Hewitt took it because of the strained relations that had to exist between those two fugitives whose trail they were following. They would be tense as banjo strings, thinking only of flight rather than strategy. For all they knew, it might be fifty men, not just two, behind them.

Count on them to keep pushing, pushing in flight, as hard as their much-abused horses could take them. Hewitt's and Mac's own horses were showing the strain a little—what must it be for the worn-out crow baits Sanderson and Fraser were riding?

Mac hauled in his horse and looked back, shaking his head. In front of them lay a narrow, stony trail probably cut by mule trains from the mines in the old days, twenty years ago, and not used much since then. On the right the bank rose only eight or ten feet, but it was too steep to climb. To the left there was a sheer drop of three to four hundred feet, all rock.

Far down there, a cold creek glittered in the shade. To a thirsty man like Hewitt it looked wonderful; only if you *fell* all that way, particularly if your feet were in a pair of stirrups, you'd be in no shape to enjoy it.

"Me help you up there," Mac said, pointing to the low cliff above them. "You watch and keep horses. Me go see."

Hewitt did not like to let, or even ask, a man who worked for him take the post of danger, but this Apache was different. Suggest that he remain behind, and he would probably get huffy and head for home.

Hewitt scrambled up the bank, Mac helping his feet find toeholds, boosting him with a lift now and then. It was perilous footing here, but the Apache would not have hesitated and Hewitt dared not in front of him. He scrambled the last few feet on his belly, holding his breath and digging in with his fingers.

He reached a sort of saddle and got on it. When he looked down he was surprised to see that he was no more than ten or twelve feet above the trail. Mac nodded his satisfaction.

Mac tied the two horses' reins together and looped them over a snag rock, so they would at least think they were tied. There was no room for them to do more than just stand there anyway, and even Sweetie had grown trail-smart this afternoon. Mac turned and went walking slowly up the narrow trail.

He vanished from Hewitt's sight a couple of times, taking sharp switchbacks. He walked slowly, bent forward, his hand on the butt of his gun.

Suddenly he reappeared, walking fast and waving for Hewitt to come to him. Hewitt swung a leg over the crest of the bare perch he occupied and called back, "Oh, no! You come help me down."

Mac almost broke into a run. He put his hands up and Hewitt threw his body over so that he hung legs down. He let go and started sliding, catching at anything with his hands. Nothing had ever felt better than those powerful hands of the Apache's catching his bootheels.

He dropped to the trail. Mac untied the horses and handed Sweetie's reins to Hewitt. "You come see this," he said. "This is one smart som'bitch."

There was no use asking questions. Hewitt followed on foot, leading Sweetie, while Mac dragged his tired horse in front. In a few feet the trail widened.

"Tie here," said Mac, "and then you come see."

Again they tied the horses. They went on foot around a sharp switchback bare of any vegetation, with the canyon wall below them almost a perpendicular wall of rock. They rounded the corner and Mac stopped and pointed ahead.

There was a rope double-half-hitched around a rock on the right and angling sharply, tautly down at about a forty-five-degree angle over the edge. It was unnecessary to ask what was on the other end of it. Neither was it necessary to proceed cautiously. The wide-open trail was visible for three hundred yards ahead.

It was Slim Fraser hanging there with a tight loop

around his neck, and when they hauled him up he was dead but his body still was not cold. It was not hard to imagine what had happened. Those "signal shots" they had fired had given Frank Sanderson his chance.

"No shootin' now," he'd say. "They's right on our trail. We cain't take no chances. Let me go ahead and see what's around the corner yander."

Slim would stop and wait nervously, unafraid of Frank's gun for the first time today, but still not feeling exactly sure of himself. In a minute, Frank would reappear, waving.

"All clear! Bring my horse and come on."

And Slim would ride ahead, into the most dangerous weapon of all. The loop would settle down around his neck before he even saw it coming. Maybe Frank had shied a rock at Slim's horse and yelled at the same time.

Anyway he did it, he had pulled Slim from the saddle and kicked him over the edge, snubbing the rope around the snag to make sure Slim lit hard enough to break his neck. He was not even taking chances that Slim could catch the rope before it choked him to death, and climb back up.

Only then he had been in too big a hurry, too scared, to cut Slim loose and let him and the rope drop out of sight. He had taken both horses and hurried on. Now he could rest one horse while he rode the other—and the $711.88 was all his.

∞∞∞

All he had to do was get safely to where he could safely spend it. The picture of the man came back vividly to

Hewitt. Frank Sanderson was brilliant in his way, but he had worse than a slight twist in his brain. He was a homicidal maniac, shrewdly sadistic, wily, implacable. The thought of him being married to a decent, sensitive girl like Charlotte was sheer horror.

And it was something to worry about even yet. She had been so young! The marks he had left on her would go deep. Could she ever recover from it? Would she ever learn ordinary human relationships—to love, to trust, to be happy with someone else? Or would there always be that secret residue of fear, suspicion and shame?

The last rays of the sun were behind them now. Frank Sanderson, looking back, would have the sun in his eyes. Well, they were entitled to one bit of luck, and Mac suddenly decided to take advantage of it. He mounted and kicked his horse into a fast walk up the naked, rocky trail.

Behind him, Sweetie obeyed perfectly as Hewitt did the same. Ahead, he saw the trail vanish around another switchback to the right. Again he felt, strongly, one of those hunches that he dared not ignore. This was the summit, Frank's last chance to get above them and shoot them out of the saddle.

"Hold it, Mac," he said.

Mac reined in and looked back. "How?"

"You keep the horses," Hewitt said. "I'm going over the top on foot."

"You figger him waitin' there?"

"He's a damn fool if he's not, Mac. We've got him outgunned, we've got the best horses, and I don't think he's over that concussion yet. He's at the end of his rope, and it's now or never."

Mac looked up, one quick glance that told him all he had to know. He slid out of the saddle and reached for Sweetie's reins, and Hewitt dismounted, picked his path, and began climbing.

Chapter Fourteen

It looked bad enough from below and it was worse than it looked. Not so much as a quarter-inch shrub grew in the thin soil on this rock spine of the mountains. He had to tuck the .45 in his shirt front and snake it every inch, choosing his route by inches, lurching ahead a foot at a time and hoping the earth did not slide out from under him.

He reached the top and then could not see the trail on either side. For all he knew, Frank Sanderson was up here with him, hidden in a crease in the bare crest, waiting for him to come closer. And there was nothing he could do but keep going.

He started slowly down the other side and suddenly saw a horse's head—a brown horse with a white face. It was a tired, dejected horse, but it had heard him and raised its head for a look around. A shiver of apprehension went through him and he froze to the ground and just hoped.

The tired horse dropped its head. He waited a moment and then crawled on down a few more feet. And suddenly he could see the entire trail, and not just the horse but Frank Sanderson, too.

His hunch had been right, and his judgment too. Frank

had looped the reins of his horse around an outcropping of rock and had started back on foot. It had been a good idea, hide on the switchback and kill them as they came around it on the narrow trail where they could not even turn their horses to run.

Only halfway there the ache in his head had caught up with him, and he had sat down and rested his elbows on his knees and his head in his hands. The right one still held the .45, but he clutched his head as though expecting it to explode with pain. He was absolutely motionless, frozen by agony in an attitude of total dejection.

How long it would last—who knew? Hewitt took a chance and scrambled a dozen feet down the slope, freezing on his belly where he would have to raise his head to see Frank. He could hear the horse's tired snort of surprise, but only one.

He raised his head and saw that the horse had lost interest. He raised it a little higher and saw Frank still sitting there in the same position. That was what concussion did to a man. That was the kind of injury that needed rest and absolute quiet. Otherwise it could leave a man with permanent brain damage, paralysis, addled wits at the very least or, if he were lucky, death during prolonged coma.

And here was this fool out here in the mountains, still trying to live his dream of being a badman, a gunnie, a terror. There he sat, a damaged, half man consumed by hatred for the man who had conquered the horse that had dumped him on the top of his head on a pebble. Behind him, nothing but savage retribution—ahead, with luck, only survival.

Hewitt slid downward a few feet more. The tired horse neither saw nor heard him. Now he could hear as well as see Frank, who put his left hand back to squeeze the back of his neck.

"Oh, Christ! Just when I need to feel good—but if I set here, mebbe it'll go away again," he said.

He began tenderly massaging his own neck, in imitation of the treatment Hewitt had given him. It was the right thing to do, but it would take forever and he did not have forever. Hewitt slid down a little farther and twisted his body so that his feet were below him. The horse looked up, trying to spot the source of the curious noise it had heard. It could not do so, and again lost interest.

It hurt too much. Frank stopped rubbing his neck and tried lying back against the rock wall, his head against it to take its weight off his neck. It must have helped because he closed his eyes and relaxed with the gun, still gripped in his right hand, in his lap.

Hewitt let himself start sliding. He brought himself to a stop and took another look. Now the horse had him spotted and had looked up, shooting its ears forward. He lay still, and it worked. The horse was too tired to sustain any alarm it felt, and Frank Sanderson was feeling too much relief to think about anything else.

Carefully, because he needed both hands and both feet to hang on, Hewitt slipped the .45 out of his shirt front and examined it. It had collected dust that he did not like, and he took his time cleaning it. He broke it open and wiped each cartridge on his shirt.

He spun the cylinder and worked the action silently a few times. He reloaded and turned on his back and took one last look at Frank Sanderson before holstering the gun. Frank had at last found a comfortable position. The pain had eased. He might even be dozing.

Hewitt dug his elbows in to secure himself. It was a good eight-foot drop to a rock-strewn trail, and momentum could take him right on over the edge.

He simply let himself start sliding, letting the friction of his back slow him down. He jumped the last four feet and landed on his feet in the trail. He whirled to face Frank with the .45 in his hand.

The horse blasted a snort of alarm and went back to the end of its reins. Now Hewitt could not see Frank, with the horse between them. He began walking swiftly forward, holding his hand out to the horse. It recognized him for a familiar man-creature and had no sense of alarm. He slapped it gently on the side to move it over against the wall, and walked swiftly past it.

Now he was within a hundred feet of Frank, who seemingly had heard or seen nothing, who still lay with his thudding head against a rock, his .45 in his hand in his lap.

Hewitt stopped. "Frank!" he called, sharply.

Frank gave no sign that he had heard. "Frank!" Hewitt said, more loudly. "Get up on your hind legs, you son-of-a-bitch. You can go either way. There's an Apache behind you and me here. Take your pick."

When Frank did not answer, Hewitt began walking toward him. Maybe, he thought, the son-of-a-bitch is dead, or at least in coma. He had a bad one, and he has pushed himself to the limit . . .

He was no more than forty feet from the man when

Frank uncoiled like a snake, lighting on his feet with his legs wide apart and his body bent to create the smallest possible target. He was, Hewitt saw in that last split-second, a big, good-looking devil. There was intelligence behind those icy blue eyes. He could have amounted to something.

Hewitt's hand dipped down toward the gun on his waistband. He caught the familiar butt in his hand and gave it the twist that freed it from his own trick-shooter's holster. He tilted it toward Frank and squeezed the trigger once.

Frank's .45 was already in his hand but more than concussion had paralyzed him. The look on his face said, "You? You? Don't I ever get free of you?" The slug hit him in the chest, blowing his heart to pieces, and he fell forward on his own gun without getting off a shot.

"Hey, Mac!" Hewitt shouted. "I got him."

Mac came around the corner of the trail, letting his own horse walk ahead of him and leading Sweetie. He caught his horse where the trail widened enough and led them up to stand looking down at Frank Sanderson's body.

"One shot," he said. "Damn good shootin'. Him plenty bad."

"Not really," said Hewitt. "It's an act. He was just pretty good. I'm better."

They left the body where it had fallen and led Frank's horse warily around it to the switchback where they could see both ways. They fired a signal every now and then and got an answering volley from the posse. But it was two hours before the sheriff and his men got there. They had Slim Fraser's horse with them. Frank had not even been able to keep an extra, worn-out horse.

"We seen them other two bodies," the sheriff said, "so now there's nobody left but Frank. Lord knows, though, he's pizen enough."

"Not even him," said Hewitt. "I just killed him. Come on, I'll show you."

"You're Hewitt?"

Hewitt handed him one of his business cards. "Oh, yes," said Rush. "We got a wire from your office offering five thousand reward for Frank. Well, well! So you're a pardner, air you?"

"Yes, I am."

"And you'll pay the reward to yourself. How about the others? Ain't there a reward on them?"

"Frank killed all four of them, Sheriff," said Hewitt, "but I don't imagine his estate would qualify to collect even if it was probated. How many of you are there? My company does the right thing."

"Fourteen beside myself."

"Suppose we say a hundred apiece. Or make it two hundred for you and a hundred and a quarter apiece for your men. I'll guarantee that, and I still have to collect our own reward. Sometimes they weasel out, you know."

"How I do know it! Mr. Hewitt, Jim Pollock says you're a gentleman and I reckon he's right. You don't really owe us nothing, and I know it."

The sheriff knew this country. It was easier to ride down the slope to a small park with a free-flowing spring than to seek a better camping place. The posse had brought a packhorse with plenty of grub, and they now could safely build a big fire. And even Mac felt at home with this bunch.

Hewitt always went out of his way to make friends with the local law, and this tired, wise, tough old sheriff was a good one. They sat talking until late at night, until fatigue finally caught up with Hewitt.

"I've got to hit the shucks, Aubrey," he said, at last. "I won't be worth shooting tomorrow if I don't catch up on my rest a little."

"Sure, sure. Could I ask you one thing, first?"

"Of course."

"Does it bother you, killing a man?"

"It might if it was a man. But Frank Sanderson? No. He was something less than human."

"I had to shoot a sixteen-year-old kid once and I felt the same way. I figgered I just saved him a life of misery and the lives of the men he would've killed if he'd lived. This is one hell of a business to be in, Mr. Hewitt, where you've got to make decisions like that."

"And then live with them the rest of your life," said Hewitt. "All I can say is that I sleep well."

"I don't know who's got a better right to," said the sheriff.

Chapter Fifteen

They all slept deeply. Hewitt was not the first to awaken. The old sheriff was up, stirring up the fire, when he got out of his blankets.

"Forgot to give you this," Rush said, taking a folded, yellow envelope from his pocket. "It came just as we left. Hope it ain't important."

It was a telegram from Hewitt's partner, Conrad Meuse, and it said:

> GET PIX ALL SUSPECTS WHEN IN CUSTODY DOA STOP
> FORWARD COPIES ME TO CIRCULATE STOP MAY BE
> OTHER CASES SAYS BIG Q STOP IMPORTANT TAKE
> PERSONAL CHARGE STAGE LOOT.

Rush was curious, and he could get a copy of the wire from the station agent anyway; so Hewitt handed it to him. "DOA" might mean "Dead on Arrival" at a city emergency hospital to the metropolitan police; to Hewitt and Conrad and many a frontier lawman it meant "Dead or Alive." "Big Q" was Johnny Quillen, head of security for the Santa Fe, a good detective, big and smart and tough, and perhaps Hewitt's closest friend. Undoubtedly Johnny had a couple of unsolved stick-ups on his log, and had correctly assumed that Hewitt was not going to seek out merely the survivor of the three man NEAT stage job.

"Is there a good photographer in Kehoe Mesa?" he asked Rush.

"Happens to be," the sheriff said. "They come and they go, but right now we got one of the best."

Rush would haul the four bodies in while Hewitt went after Pat Herndon, probably with the help of Mac. "Have him get the most lifelike pictures possible of these stiffs, will you?" said Hewitt. "Make me plenty of copies. I won't quarrel about his bill."

Mac came out of the brush where he had slept apart, still shy about fraternizing with the white law. Rush had coffee on. Hewitt mixed ash-cakes from corn meal and water and baked them on a flat stone while Rush broiled bacon.

Long before daylight, long before the posse was ready to travel, Hewitt and Mac slipped off on their private hunt. So far as anyone knew, the only criminal charge against Pat Herndon was his attack on Hewitt and Mac, and he might be able to defend himself against that by pleading self-defense. They had, after all, attacked him first. His seduction and sale of Charlotte was ancient history and an old, grubby story that they would not want to drag through a court of law anyway.

"One thing we're all forgetting," said Rush, as the two mounted.

"What's that?" Hewitt asked.

"The forty thousand from the stage robbery. You killed the one man who knew where it was."

"I sort of doubt that," said Hewitt. "One thing at a

time, Sheriff. We'll come back to it before we're through."

"You know where it is."

"I've got a hunch, is all."

The sheriff did not quite know how to say it. "I was a deputy marshal for a long time. Lost my job when we changed Presidents. I ain't as young as I used to be. I don't care about the reward. But I do care about some Pinkerton comin' in here and findin' that money right under my nose and makin' me look foolish. All I know is the law game, and jobs ain't that easy to find."

"Just go back and tell them you're playing a hunch. That's all any of us can do. Results are what count, anyway."

Rush still was not happy, but he knew when to push and when to take off the pressure. He gave them a good-luck wave as they walked their horses quietly out of camp, letting Rush's tired men sleep.

They had a disagreeable job ahead of them. Somebody was going to have to ride double, to let one fairly docile horse carry two bodies—until they came to the other two. Then four of his possemen would have to double up on two horses.

Again Hewitt let Mac lead the way. The Apache picked an easy route that saved the horses and got them to where they had left Pat Herndon, bootless, unarmed and wounded, a couple of hours after daylight. There were the ashes of Herndon's fire. There was the place where he and Hewitt had disturbed the brush and the dirt, fighting.

But there was no Herndon.

Mac got down and studied the trail a long time, shaking his head. Hewitt dismounted too, but he said nothing. The Indian would communicate what he thought was important in his own good time. They plodded along together for nearly half an hour.

Hewitt thought he could see where Herndon had dragged himself along on hands and knees, with more guts than Hewitt had thought he possessed. Then Mac showed him where he had found first one staff and then another, so he could get up and walk. Not fast, not easily, but still it was better than crawling.

And, as straight as he could, he had been heading for the cabin to which Jim and Hewitt had taken Charlie "because nobody knew about it." That had been a mistake. It would be strange indeed if so isolated a stout little house remained unknown to men looking for a hideout. They had taken too much for granted.

And it worried Hewitt when he thought of Dick Easton there alone, with a wound in his side. True, he had the Winchester '73, but he had to sleep sometime, and he would not be expecting an attack from a perfect stranger.

Once they knew where they were going they could mount up and make better time. When the sign of Herndon's trail vanished, Mac did not worry. He pushed on, and soon picked it up and pointed it out to Hewitt again. So far he had not said one word, but he had proved he knew his job as few men did.

Long before midday they came in sight of the cabin. They circled it, keeping to the trees, and approached from behind. Joe Dunn's body remained in plain sight from here on the top of the shed, undisturbed. In an hour or so, coming from the north by the most direct trail, the posse would arrive to pick it up and take it to Kehoe Mesa.

What interested Hewitt was the big back window in the back room. It was no hunch that Herndon was there, because they had trailed him there. What they did not know was whether Easton still had the Winchester or Herndon had managed to take it away from him.

The most disturbing thing was the absence of the dog. It had refused to follow Charlie off with the Apaches and had skulked off into the brush instead. It had plainly adopted this cabin as home, and at this time of day should be in sight somewhere, ready to mooch his breakfast.

It was not necessary to explain the significance of the big back window to Mac. He saw it too. If it was Herndon, he still had not left the cabin because Dick Easton's horse still stood in the corral.

For a long time they watched, standing in the timber beside their horses. Mac could be as patient as he had to be, but Hewitt found the time crawling. The last of the deer flies, the ones that had survived the frost, had come out with the sun and were making life miserable for them and the horses. Only Mac seemed able to ignore them.

And then Hewitt muttered, "Damn!" Which said it all. A man had come to the big window, carrying a Winchester '73 which, Hewitt knew, was loaded with the new, smokeless powder. And it was not Dick Easton.

Herndon stood there a long time. He knew he was vulnerable despite the range of the gun because he could watch only one side of the house at a time. It would keep him awake and worried and on the move.

"What'll we do, Mac?" Hewitt asked. "For all we know, there's a wounded man still alive in there. We can't just smoke him out."

"Him go soon," Mac said. "Him not wait for be caught here. How we steal horse?"

It made sense. Hewitt, who knew the ground, thought it over.

"Tell you what, Mac. We'll slip down there together. I'll show you where to hide where you can cover front and back, whichever way he comes out. I think I can take a couple of poles out of the corral farthest from the house, and not be seen. If I am, you'll have him at short range."

Mac merely nodded. They tied their horses and circled widely through the brush, descending into a shallow canyon and climbing out of it far above the cabin. Still no smoke arose from the kitchen stovepipe. Charlie had not taken all the provisions with her, yet for some reason Herndon was not taking time to fix a breakfast. Maybe he had cooked his traveling rations yesterday.

They got down on their knees to approach the cabin from the rear. Easton's horse scented them and whickered in friendly fashion. They froze. In a moment, Herndon came hobbling out the front door, carrying the Winchester in his left hand and supporting himself on a staff.

Every step looked painful. If his foot had improved any, it did not show from here. He was at the extreme range of a .45, but only in the direst circumstances would Hewitt have tried a shot as long as Herndon had the Winchester.

The horse had lost interest in Hewitt and Mac and gone back to feeding. Herndon painfully hobbled back into the house. He would keep a sharp eye on that horse, with his foot in that shape.

"You take back window and I take front door," Mac whispered. "Smoke the som'bitch out."

"We can't, so long as there's a chance Dick Easton is alive in there," Hewitt replied. "We've got to take him outside. First we turn the horse loose."

They crept forward again, and this time they were ignored by the horse. Hewitt did not know how good Mac was with a strange .45, and to be able to see both the front door and the back window left him with a long shot. Mac did not seem to worry about it, a good sign.

Mac lay on his belly and crawled into the evergreen brush where he was invisible even to Hewitt. Hewitt stood up and, darting swiftly from tree to tree, approached the back of the corral. The last tree left him a good fifteen feet away from cover of any kind.

The corral was built of heavy poles anchored deeply in the ground, with horizontal poles, five of them, fastened to the uprights. The two bottom poles were wired, but the three top ones merely lay on pegs driven into holes drilled into the posts inside the corral.

No way to tell when it was safe to do so; so he left the cover of the tree and walked swiftly to the corral. He lifted off the top pole and lowered it quietly to the ground. The horse saw him and came over to watch. He lifted off the next pole. It, too, went down without making a sound.

He heard a warning hiss from Mac and simply kicked

the third pole down. It fell with a clatter and something smashed into his left arm as he raced back toward the cover of the tree. He heard the boom of the Winchester before he felt the wave of pain and saw the blood start running down his arm.

He got out his pocket knife and cut off the sleeve. The big .44 slug had left an ugly wound on the outer muscles, but it had missed the bone by a wide margin.

And the shot had spooked the horse into jumping the two remaining bars of the corral. It did not run very far, however. It was a curious, friendly, well-broken horse, and Mac knew as well as Hewitt did that Herndon could probably hobble close enough to it with a piece of bread to get a rope on it.

Mac came snaking backward out of the brush and got up on one knee. He laid the .45 across his left wrist to steady it and fired once. The slug hit the horse in the tip of one of its ears. Startled and in pain, it whirled and raced off into the timber, shaking its head until it was out of sight.

Herndon had come out in plain sight to fire the shot, but when he heard Mac's .45 he ducked back behind the corner of the house. And if we're in bad shape to get at him, Hewitt thought angrily, gritting his teeth at the waves of pain from his torn arm, he's in a bad spot himself. He has to get away and we don't . . .

He and Mac did not have to talk over plans. They thought alike. They began walking swiftly down toward the corner of the cabin behind which Herndon had retreated. Mac split to the right, to cover their rear in case

Herndon came out the big back window. Hewitt lurked at the very corner of the cabin.

Now the throb in his arm was like fire, and he knew that shock alone could soon make his whole body undependable. He held his breath and listened and could hear Herndon's heavy breathing no more than a couple of feet away. The lout was scared stiff. What good was his long gun when his targets vanished so quickly?

Hewitt holstered his gun, hearing the faint click as the catch in the holster engaged the front sight. He took out the sap and waited, and in a moment the barrel of the Winchester came snaking out from behind the corner.

He jumped and grabbed it with his left hand and shouted. Herndon was tremendously strong and this was Hewitt's bad arm, but one grunt brought Mac to his side. Mac got hold of the Winchester just as it went off into the ground, but he held the barrel pointed downward with both hands.

Hewitt stepped around the building in plain sight. He saw Herndon let go of the rifle and go for a .45 in his pocket. Hewitt smiled and said, "Oh no, I don't think so!"

He leaped and snapped the cosh as hard as he could. He caught Herndon on the left cheekbone and ripped it open without knocking him out. Herndon groped for him with both hands.

Hewitt stood his ground and let the big fellow come at him. He feinted for the face and then rapped Herndon sharply on the right wrist. Herndon's arm came down and Hewitt went for the temple.

He connected solidly enough to kill a man with a softer head. Herndon simply collapsed. Mac leaped to his feet, holding the cherished Winchester lovingly. Hewitt raced into the cabin.

Dick Easton was lying in a corner of the front room, near the cold stove. His face was a mess. He could barely see through either eye, but he was alive and in a mean mood.

"Mr. Hewitt!" he exclaimed.

Hewitt dropped to his knee beside him. "How are you, Dick?"

"He just beat the hell out of me. Snuck up behind me when I went out to the woodpile and banged me over the head with something. Next thing I knowed, he had me down on the floor here and was banging away with his fists and saying, 'Where is it? Where is it?' I'm sore all over."

"We're in the same shape, Dick," said Hewitt. "I prescribe a good, long rest for both of us."

"Yes," said Dick, "but what the hell was he after me for when he kept askin' 'Where is it?' What did he mean?"

"Forty thousand dollars," said Hewitt.

Chapter Sixteen

Herndon was unconscious for nearly an hour, during which Hewitt, one-armed, tried to repair again some of the damage to his foot. Now there were some broken bones and some bad inflammation. There was not much he could do, and he thought it was even money that a doctor would have to amputate the whole foot.

Herndon came out of it moaning and weeping. When he realized where he was and what had happened, he lay back and closed his eyes. They had not tried to put him on the bed. The two of them together were not capable of handling the big fellow because of the wounds they had received from him, and neither felt much like trying.

But until he did regain consciousness, Hewitt did his best with the foot. If Herndon lost it, he would always blame Hewitt. One more enemy, Hewitt thought bitterly, in a lifetime of collecting them, and always from the same kind of people . . .

When they heard the sheriff's posse coming, he sent Mac off to bring Charlie back to Jim Pollock's place. "I want all four of you to come," he said. "I owe you people a lot, and I want to square it with you."

"They don't come," said Mac. "Bastardly cattlemen, they don't like Apaches."

Hewitt shook his fist under Mac's nose. "You're talking about a friend of mine," he said. "If he's not good enough for Apaches, to hell with you. Tell the old man that. Tell him I dare him to come!"

Mac rode off, kicking his tired old bone-bag of a horse into a shambling trot. Hewitt waited impatiently for the posse. His wounded arm was swelling and the pain was intense at times. Even a shallow wound could turn gangrenous and cost him an arm.

They were a sorry-looking lot, going down the mountain. Hewitt found himself unable to control Sweetie with his bad arm, and had to trade horses with another man. Two men rode double and two horses each carried two corpses.

Pat Herndon, still dazed and in shock, still maintaining not a stubborn silence but a stupid one, rode the packhorse that had carried the posse's provisions. He was perched precariously on top of what was left of them, his feet connected by a rope under the horse's belly. It was neither comfortable nor very safe, but he did as he was told, obeying like a man who knew he had nothing to lose.

"Which makes me wonder," Hewitt confided to Sheriff Rush, as they rode down the canyon, "if maybe he wasn't into some kind of deviltry before he left Kehoe Mesa. He's not in serious trouble that I know of. As far as I'm concerned, thirty days in the clink will fix him up for attacking me."

"Nothing that I know of," Rush said. "Maybe he pulled a job in Prescott that we haven't heard about yet. He sure ain't causing no trouble, is he?"

"I escorted a man to his own hanging once, who acted just like that," said Hewitt. "As though drunk, too drunk to think. As though loaded with opium. An ox, silent and slow to respond.

"Only at the last minute he realized what was happening and went crazy. It took five men to hold him and he hurt one of them pretty bad before they got him hanged."

"We'll watch him," said Rush. "I'm so damn tired, I ain't in the mood for no nonsense. Bend an oak doubletree over his haid if he gits smart."

⊕⊕⊕

Rush sent a man ahead to the Dot 4 Dot as they reached level ground and asked Jim to bring wagons and extra horses. By then, Hewitt's arm was hurting intolerably and he felt feverish. If it was an infection it had come on faster than he had ever seen one come. Rush had also asked Jim to send for the doctor, and this was all that was on Hewitt's mind.

It was dark before the wagon got to them. It was a heavy spring wagon with an upholstered seat and a deep box. Rush unceremoniously stacked all five corpses in it. Hewitt gave up and got on the seat beside the driver. He did not have to tell the man to crack it to the team.

Any man who lived as much by the gun as he did had to expect things like this, and he thought he had grown philosophical about it. He had looked death in the eye many a time without flinching; in fact, the greatest gamble of all was one of the attractions of this game. But to face losing an arm at his age, thanks to a damned half-wit like Herndon, was morbidly depressing.

Jim Pollock, riding beside another wagon, met them shortly. Learning that the other wagon would not be needed, he told the driver to turn around and head for home.

"If that goddamn doctor ain't there yet, send somebody to bring him in at gunpoint," he said. "Tell Edna to get a bed ready and boil up plenty of water and keep it boiling."

"Yes, there are two of us with gunshot wounds," Hewitt said.

"I don't give a damn about the other one," Jim said. "I'd like to drag him home at the end of a rope around his bad leg, is what I'd like to do."

Lamps and lanterns twinkled all over the ranch, making it visible long before they got there. When they rode into the yard, Jim pointed to a handsome top buggy whose team was tied near the door of the house. "Doc's here, anyway," he said. "And he's pretty good. Learned most of his medicine in the Army, in the Indian wars, and then went to college to make sure he had it right. You cain't fool him on a wound."

They had to help Hewitt into the house and put him to bed. Jim had a patented lamp that burned naphtha under pressure. He claimed it took a mechanic to run it, which was why he did not often fire it up, but he lighted it for the doctor to examine Hewitt's wound as they sat together on the side of the bed.

"This is no rifle wound," the doctor said.

"The hell it's not. I saw him shoot me," said Hewitt.

"We'll see. I'm going to have to cut into it and you're

going to have to take chloroform. I got ether but you can't use it at night in this damnable primitive country because it's so flammable. Jim, get a table ready."

They put three or four quilts on the big dining table and helped Hewitt up on it. Before he took the chloroform he said, "Jim, there'll be four Apaches coming in with Charlie sometime or other. I want to talk to them if you can hold them here that long. If you can't, I want them given four good horses. I'll pay you for them."

"All right, what else?"

"Just thank them, in my name, for taking care of Charlie. And ask Aubrey Rush if he'll write out some kind of pass for them so they won't be molested before they get home because they'll be riding good horses and that's an easy way for some thieving lawman to help himself to them."

"They'll have bills of sale."

"Not for payment for anything! I don't think you could pay them for what they've done. They'd just get insulted. This is a gift from a friend."

Jim put his hand against Hewitt's chest and said, "Lay down. Are you goin' to try to learn me about Apaches? Hell, I fought 'em for nine years!"

When Hewitt came to he was back in bed, his arm was bandaged and in a sling, and the doctor was dozing on a chair beside the bed. He awakened at the first sound Hewitt made.

He picked up something from the small table nearby.

"So this is a rifle bullet, is it?" he said. "This is what I had to cut out of your arm."

It was a hardwood splinter, wedge-shaped, half an inch square at the thick end and tapering down to a bladelike edge in an inch. Hewitt tried to examine it.

"Turn the light up," he said.

"All right," the doctor grumbled, "but I know wood when I see it, and that's no rifle bullet."

"Look," said Hewitt, when the light was brighter, "this side of the wood is weathered and the other side is bright and clean. He nicked the corral pole shooting at me, and the slug carried that piece along with it."

The doctor scratched his chin. "I remember taking a half-inch horn button out of a rifle wound once. Bullet went right on through and the button wasn't even marked. Was a lieutenant, and he had it mounted in gold for his wife to wear as a breast pin, because that's where it hit him, in the chest."

"There you are."

"Well, I done the best I could for you, young man. I laid that arm open and swabbed it good with a phenol solution. No veins or arteries or important nerves damaged but you've got some muscles that will be a right smart spell healing. Now I'm going to give you something to make you sleep."

Hewitt held up his hand. "Wait a minute, how long have I been asleep?"

"Say an hour and a half."

"The Apaches haven't shown up with the girl yet?"

"No," said the doctor, "and there's nothing you could

do if they did. Ever take laudanum? Open your mouth.
That's an order, rookie!"

The laudanum was already taking effect before Hewitt
remembered Pat Herndon. His tongue was thick, his wits
wooly, and he was glad to see Jim Pollock come into the
room.

"Herndon," he managed to say. "How's his foot?"

"I wish to hell I knowed," Jim said, gloomily. "Would
you believe, Jeff, that he got away?"

"How?"

"My fault."

Hewitt's control of his own mind was slipping rapidly.
He had to make a concentrated effort to take in what Jim
was saying.

Herndon had been operated on right after the doctor
got through with Hewitt's arm. He had a broken metatarsal bone, but he refused anesthesia and made the doctor
fish up and join the pieces, and then make a cast of thick
adobe mud, well wrapped in muslin. He let them carry
him out to the barn then, where Aubrey Rush personally
chained his good leg to a post supporting the roof.

It was Edna who insisted that he be given a straw tick
to sleep on, not just a pile of straw. All who had ridden
with Rush's posse were dead tired; many were sleeping
wherever they could find a soft, secluded place to sleep.
Jim had a reliable cowboy by the name of Lincoln Tasho
he could trust to do the job.

Aubrey tossed Link Tasho the key to the padlock to
Herndon's chain. "In case you have to tighten it, not
loosen it," he said. "If he gits a straw tick to sleep on he
can sleep on a shorter chain."

"Yes, sir," said Tasho.

"I made sure there's nothing within reach he can get hold of for a weapon, but watch him, Link. He don't act like no normal man to me."

Tasho went out. He did not come back, but no one noticed for nearly an hour. When they went to look for him in the bunkhouse, no one had seen him.

He was just getting to his knees when they ran pellmell to the barn with a lantern. Herndon had not bothered to fake anything. He put one arm around the pole to which he was chained and hoisted himself up so Link could put the straw tick down. Link stooped to do so.

Still clinging to the pole, Herndon swung his other fist. He caught Tasho on the temple and he kept going down. Tasho thought that Herndon hit him again, but that was all he knew. When he awakened, he was on his face on the straw tick and Herndon was gone.

So were the padlock and chain.

"That's what puzzles me," Pollock said. "What's he want with them?"

"It doesn't puzzle me," said Hewitt. "He knows we've sent for Charlie, and he's insane where she's concerned. Did he get away with a horse?"

"As good a horse as I've got."

"Gun?"

"A thirty-calibre Henry carbine."

Hewitt tried to sit up but the drug's effect was already too deep. He fell back in bed, mumbling, "Go after him. He'll snipe down all four of those Apaches and treat her worse than Frank Sanderson did."

He thought Jim said something before going out, but he had no idea what it was. He slept.

Chapter Seventeen

Arizona! Sitting in Jim Pollock's big cowhide rocking chair, his feet up and his arm throbbing in a sling, Jeff Hewitt had plenty of time to reflect on his own introduction to the Territory's bloody history. He had been new to Allen Pinkerton's organization then, a green kid who did not have sense enough to be scared. He had worked his way into a gang of hard-working horse thieves who proved that crime did pay, but not easily. Half that much hard work, half that much planning and risk and organization, would have made them rich men.

Instead, they were pelting across the flat, open desert as hard as their fine, stolen mounts would go—five of them, with thirteen Apaches behind them. Hewitt remembered the sound of arrows even though, thanks to the difference in the horses, they fell far short.

How relieved his four thieving companions had been to see a squadron of cavalry! The Apaches saw them in time, saw they were badly outnumbered and outgunned, and retreated. The troopers let them go but gave the five men hell for venturing into what was known to be a war zone.

"It wasn't our idea exactly, Captain," Hewitt said. He opened his shirt and took out the sweatproof packet he wore on a string around his belly. He thumbed it open and took out his Pinkerton credentials.

"Some prevaricating scoundrel said there would be a column of remount horses on this trail tonight. I don't know how these rumors get around, but I'm arresting these men for three prior thefts and one shooting, and I'm officially requesting you to take custody of them."

He had been prone to use big words then, and to milk a situation of rather too much drama. But even then he had been a good detective, and he had known it, and he knew it now.

And now he had to sit—thirty endless hours of idleness so far—and depend on others to do his work. Jim Pollock was out on his big gray, Slocum, with most of his gang, hoping to intercept the Apaches with Charlie before Pat Herndon could ambush them. Sheriff Rush had called the photographer to come out and take pictures of the five dead men, and was now on his way to Prescott with their bodies.

Dick Easton had not only a wound in his side, he had been beaten to a pulp by Herndon. His eyes were half-closed, his mouth was swollen, and his nose broken. But he could not be kept in bed. He hobbled about the place on a makeshift cane, feeding Edna's chickens for her, picking the last tomatoes in the garden—and going crazy with worry over Charlie.

Poor Arizona! So much riches but so hard to get at that it took hard men to harvest them. The mines and forests and grassy mesas had been fought over again and again. Every spot that had a name represented what had once been believed a source of riches, and there were few that did not have bloody episodes in their history.

Hewitt got out of the rocking chair and found he could

get around without pitching forward on his face. The
heavy dose of laudanum had worn off. The doctor had
left instructions with Edna for him to stay off his feet, but
the moment Charlie got here, his work would begin
whether anyone liked it or not.

He went outside, successfully evading Edna, and found
that after a little walking, the pain in his arm subsided to
a dull, pulsing ache. He supposed that meant it was healing; certainly the swelling was going down. He found
Dick Easton in the garden, searching for little green tomatoes for Edna to pickle.

"Hidy, Mr. Hewitt," Dick said. "We're a pair for sure."

"Between us," said Hewitt, "we'd make about half a
man."

Easton smiled a painful, crooked smile. "I figger I
could whup my weight in newborn kittens today."

"Dick, I'd like to talk to you about something that's
probably none of my business. You're pretty crazy about
Charlie, aren't you?"

"She sure seems like a nice woman to me," Dick said,
warily, after a brief hesitation.

"Now that's what I call real passion! That's the way to
sweep a woman off her feet. I'm not asking just to pry.
I'm interested in that girl's future."

Dick got up off his knees and said, bitterly, "What
kinda future have I got? You know how much I make
here? Thirty-five dollars a month because Jim pays me a
five-dollar bonus, and it's the best job I ever had in my
life. How can a man get married on that?"

"Many a man has, and gone on with the right wife to
become prosperous and respected."

"And still more has raised up a family of kids that have to live on biscuits and bacon gravy most of the time because their worthless father can't provide better. The wives take in washing and age fast. No, sir, not for me! I ain't doin' that to any woman."

"But suppose the woman has had such a miserable life that having a decent man, even in poverty, would be—"

Dick cut in passionately, "I know the kind of life she led, and she's got a right to the best the world can give her to make up for it. Hell, Mr. Hewitt, I kin barely read and write! How am I going to be anything but somebody else's hired hand?"

Here I go again, Hewitt thought, fixing up somebody else's life for him . . . Conrad Meuse called him a born buttinski who liked to "tidy up" things for his friends. "In the old country," said Conrad, "you'd be an *Ehestifter*. You know, of course, what that is."

"No, but I'll bet here's where I learn a new German word I'll never need."

"A professional matchmaker, an arranger of marriages for a fee between people who were perfectly all right until you came along." When Conrad got excited his accent thickened. "*Gott*, you are an imbossible egoist. Buttinski! Leave alone sometimes people ven dey are vell off."

"Sure, Conrad," said Hewitt. "Let's go to dinner, have a bottle of wine and some roast beef, and I'll introduce you to a handsome widow about your own age. Ranch of her own, money in the bank, five kids—"

Conrad had choked on his indignation and strode off. There might be a grain of truth in what he had said, but

Hewitt thought he had seen as many lives ruined by timidity as by gall.

"Charlie is just learning to write," he said. "She can read well, and she can print about as fast as I can write. But she never had a chance, either. The two of you can learn together."

"And live on what?"

"Ah, here's where we separate the men from the boys, Dick. If you're a real man you'll capture the woman—drive her crazy—make her happy—show her you idolize her—give this one, especially, back her pride as a woman. And once you have done that, then you buckle down and figure out how to support her.

"Because you always can, some way, if you're a real man. This is a good job you've got—for a kid. I'm only saying it's time you grew up. Somebody sure as hell owes that girl more than anyone has ever given her."

"Mr. Hewitt, just how the hell come you're so interested in Charlie? Why don't you marry her yourself?"

"I'm too old for her, and I'm not a marrying man. Charlie's the daughter I'd like to have, and don't."

"There you are! If she really was your daughter, would you want her to marry the likes of me?"

"I'd want to see how much of a man you were first. I know you can work, I know you can think, I know you can fight, and I know you're faithful as a soldier. But I just wonder how long you're going to go on living in Jim Pollock's bunkhouse and doing a manager's work for a five-dollar-a-month bonus."

He turned and hobbled off, leaving Dick standing there with his battered mouth open. Jim Pollock would scream like a puma if he knew about it, but he had more than he could handle here and he had no sons of his own. As Conrad would say, Hewitt was really doing him a favor he did not want done . . . yet.

Waiting was the hardest thing of all. Waiting was what got him into these situations where he tidied up other people's lives for them. Waiting—

He saw two riders coming from far away, riding bad horses at a tired trot. They vanished crossing a gully, but when they emerged again he was sure it was Mac and Charlie. He could do nothing but wait for them, leaning against a fence where he could rest his bad arm across a rail.

They were on the two poorest horses the Apaches had been riding. Charlie had stopped somewhere recently to wash her face and arms, but her shirt and Levi's were filthy. And the moment she came close to him, she began fighting to hold back the tears.

"The grandfather died last night," she said. "He has to go home, so I let them have my horse. Mac brought me back, but he has to go home too now."

All Hewitt could do was give her a hand down. She was close to the point of exhaustion. "Damn it," he said, "there are men out looking for you everywhere. Didn't anyone find you?"

"You betcha not," said Mac. "We see damn cowboy all the places, but you think they find Apache? You mus' be crazy, Hewitt."

"What happened to the old man?"

"It was a heart attack, I'm sure. He was sitting there

waiting for me to finish supper, when he just lay down on his side and was gone. Just like that," said Charlie.

"I'm sorry, Mac. He didn't look that old to me."

"Grandfather have eighty-six years. That's why we take this last ride, show him still a hell of a man, see? Now I got to go home too, and help show him the trail. I done you good favor, I like to borrow good horse instead."

"Mac, I promised all of you good horses, but Jim's not here to sign a bill of sale. Let me see if Edna can sign one."

It got a little complicated. Edna agreed to sign bills of sale, which she had done before, but she did not know what horses Jim would want to part with. Mac was drooling for the horses but eager to be gone, and at one point was ready to ride off on his half-dead and worn-out cayuse.

Then Dick Easton came limping down from the garden and took charge. "Hidy, Charlie," he said. "You let them have your horse so he only needs three. You go up to the house and tell Edna to write up bills of sale for Pansy, a three-year-old bay, Squire, a four-year-old black gelding with three white feet, and Monkey, a four-year-old buckskin gelding with one lop ear."

"I s'pose Pansy's a mare," Charlie said.

Dick did not answer. She looked at him and saw the hunger in his eyes, the respectful adoration for which he could not—now, at least—find words. Hewitt saw her face flame as she turned and hurried up to the house.

He put out his hand to Mac. "As a trouble-making Apache savage, Mac," he said, "you're a hell of a specimen of a good friend in a pinch. Where did you have her hidden out?"

"Got a cave yander." Mac made a deliberately vague gesture, as though they might need the shelter of the cave again sometime. "We didn't do nothing to make her shamed."

"You don't have to tell me that."

Mac accepted a bridle and a pair of halters with ropes, but no saddle. When Edna brought down the bills of sale describing and transferring title to the horses, there was no buyer's name filled in.

"What do you want me to put in for the new owner's name?" she asked.

"Jack Mackintosh," said Mac.

"Where'd you get that name?" Hewitt asked, as Edna inscribed it on the three bills of sale.

"He tried to kill me and I killed him, the som'bitch. I take his horse and his gun and his hat," said Mac, "and now I take his name, too."

Edna's hand jerked and made a slight mess of the one name, but she finished the job. She also gave Mac the pass that Sheriff Aubrey Rush had written out before leaving for Prescott. It stated that "four adult male Chemehuevi Indians had rendered appreciable aid to the undersigned in his duties, names unknown except that one is called Mac, and courtesy in permitting them to return peacefully to their homes will be appreciated."

Hewitt had to explain what the pass was. Mac pushed it into his pocket. "I guess it won't hurt," he said. "Listen, Hewitt—you watch out for that som'bitch Herndon. You know where Charlie and that man of hers lived?"

"Yes."

"You know what's there?"

"Yes, I know."

"Well," said Mac, "so does Herndon. I give you thanks from the grandfather and all our people."

He kicked his horse around and rode off, leading the other two at an easy canter. He did not look back.

Chapter Eighteen

"It's nowhere near that damn mine of Frank's," Jim exploded. "Do you think Aubrey Rush and Tom Coflin were half-witted, or what? They dug out ten or fifteen tons of dump there. That'd be the likeliest place to hide it, in the tailings.

"They searched every square foot for a hundred yards around. They dug up the floor and like to tore the cabin to pieces. If there's one man would keep his loot close by, where he could grab it and run, it'd be Frank Sanderson. And it ain't there."

The three men—Hewitt, Jim and Dick Easton, were enjoying fourth and fifth cups of after-supper coffee. Charlie had bathed this afternoon and then had slept for several hours. In the presence of poor Dick, who was still dressed like a tramp, unbathed and unshaven, and beaten to a pulp, she looked like a schoolgirl.

She could not keep her eyes off Dick, and yet she flushed and looked away and usually hurried out to the kitchen whenever he looked up at her. Poor kid, she had missed so much of young girlhood, and without knowing it was trying to live it now. Well, let her. There was not much she did not know about the seamy, squalid side of life. Let this schoolgirlish crush help cleanse her.

"Charlie," Hewitt said, when she came in with more coffee, "come back in and sit a minute with us. I want to ask you some questions."

"All right."

She took the coffee pot back to the kitchen. Edna came back with her to join them.

"Frank set off a pretty big dynamite shot a few days before Jim's barbecue, didn't he?" Hewitt asked.

"Yes, too big. It blocked the tunnel and he just raved because he had to haul rock for three days in a wheelbarrow before he could look at his new drift head and see if he'd found color."

"Had he?"

"He sure never told me if he did."

"How much dynamite did he use, do you know?"

"He said five sticks."

"That's a good shot. Did he have any more?"

"Oh, yes, he bought twenty sticks."

"Then he's got a powderhouse there somewhere."

"Yes."

"I can show you the powderhouse," Jim Pollock said, impatiently. "It was searched. It was empty."

"You mean no money and no dynamite."

"A spider couldn't have found enough stuff in there to make a web."

Hewitt looked back at Charlie. "Where did he get the dynamite, do you know?"

Again that look of shame, as memories of that old life overwhelmed her briefly. "There was this fellow that stole six cases up at Flagstaff last year—did you know about that?"

Hewitt shook his head, but Jim said, "I did. They never caught him."

"No. He was oh, so careful! He sold it two and three and four sticks at a time. It was the first thing he ever robbed and he was afraid of everybody. Frank had to give him thirty cents a stick."

"Six dollars cash," said Hewitt.

"Yes."

"Did you see him pay the man? Do you know what form the money was in or how much more he had?"

"No, he never let me know things like that. He told me he was broke. But he could always find money for that damn mine!"

"So there should still be fifteen sticks of dynamite in his powderhouse."

"Yes."

"Did he ever use black powder?"

"Oh no, he wouldn't have the stuff on the place. And it really ain't much good in a hardrock mine, Mr. Hewitt. Only when you can't get dynamite."

"Isn't he afraid—or wasn't he—that somebody would steal his dynamite?"

She shook her head. "No. The powderhouse is built of logs eight inches thick, underground, and then there's several tons of dirt piled on top of that. He bought a door from the old Dancing Maiden mine for it, and two padlocks."

Jim Pollock said, "That door is made of solid, six-inch oak timbers spiked on one at a time and then cross-cleated with spiked oak at the back. If you used enough dynamite to blow it open, you'd set off what he stored inside."

"But we can burn that door down. Fire won't detonate dynamite. It takes percussion—a primer. Plenty of coal oil to soak it, a little black powder to see that the fire gets a good start, plenty of water to douse it when it has burned through enough to let us pry off the padlocks—"

Down came Jim's big fist. "By God, it'll work! You learn to be so careful around dynamite, you forget that tons of it have burned up without going off."

His face fell. "But that powderhouse has been searched twice, and—"

"Before Frank put the locks on it?"

"Let's see, once before and once after. What has that got to do with it?"

"Jim, how hard would it be to stash a bundle of forty thousand dollars away in a temporary hiding place while they're ransacking his place? He lets them get a look in his powderhouse. Then he puts two big locks on it to make them suspicious. I'll bet he growled like hell when they made him unlock it."

"He sure did," said Charlie. "He said they had to have a court order. Marshal Coffin said all right, he'd leave all six men to guard the powderhouse while he rode in and got a—it had a funny name but Frank knew what it meant."

"*Subpoena duces tecum?*"

"That was it!"

"That's a court order summoning not just a person, but his records or evidence—for instance, dynamite."

"Frank said oh, all right, if they wanted to be so ornery

about it. He unlocked both locks and let them in. All he had in there was two sticks of dynamite."

"There you are, Jim. It's the only place it can be, because he'd never keep it very far from him—he'd want to be able to lay hands on it in a hurry. I'll bet you that within an hour after Deputy Marshal Coflin left, he had the swag in the powderhouse."

"Let's find out tomorrow," said Jim, "and let's don't fool with no police officers or court orders. We got Mrs. Sanderson here. She can give us permission."

They left Dick Easton behind, in charge of four good men, to guard the house and the women. They saddled up and left before daylight. At first they rode together, chatting in low voices, but as they neared the ascent to the Sanderson place, Hewitt and Jim stopped them and carefully deployed them.

Somewhere up there, Hewitt was sure, Pat Herndon would be lurking. Somehow he knew—or had at least surmised—that the loot from the North East Arizona Transport robbery was on the Sanderson property. Maybe he just had the same kind of mind, half fox and half wolf, and thought the same way Frank had.

By daylight, with the sun at their backs, they advanced up the slope in a line that spanned close to four hundred yards. Where they could not ride, they walked and led their horses. Hewitt took the well-worn trail because he thought Herndon would be watching it, and he wanted first crack at the big animal himself.

It had not been quite so cold last night, and it was

warming faster this morning. Birds that soon would be on
their way on the next leg of their southward journey were
out. So were squirrels. The bluejays that wintered here
and thought they owned everything, gave them away by
flying overhead. They swooped down on the advancing
line of men, darting at them and shrieking raucously.

The little shanty where Hewitt had first seen Charlotte
Law Sanderson came into sight, and there was still no
sign of Pat Herndon—indeed no sign that he had passed
this way. About at the end of rifle range, just in case
Herndon had got hold of another one, Hewitt pulled
Sweetie down and signaled his men to him.

The mare was behaving like a ladies' horse now, but
what she would do if gunfire started would probably be
something else. It was going to be hard to give up this
horse.

He picked out two men to make a wide circle to the
left, two to go to the right. Those on the right would be
nearer the mine, but the closer they got to it, the harder it
would be to see anything. It faced this way, a rectangular
black hole, well-cribbed with oak. The pickets would
come in with the tunnel under their feet and only the
house and grounds visible.

Someone had to help Hewitt out of the saddle and lead
Sweetie back down the trail and tie her securely by the
halter. It was just as the man returned that Hewitt and
several others saw the blaze flare up, somewhere on the
slope above them, behind the house, where the powderhouse was supposed to be. Hewitt and Jim Pollock
grinned at each other and waved to the men, *Close in,
close in.*

Herndon was too occupied with his plan and his work, too excited at the prospect of getting his hands on the money, to be as alert as he should have been. He had done exactly as Hewitt had planned. He had soaked that part of the heavy door that held the big hasps and padlocks with coal oil and set them afire. He had a sledge hammer, a crowbar and three big buckets of water to put out the fire before it could burn up the loot.

He had fashioned a crutch out of a T-shaped limb and was waiting anxiously, the sledge hammer in his right hand, as the fire bit into the pitch-pine logs. "Pass the word," Hewitt whispered. "Let him do the work, let him knock off those hasps, and then close in on him while he's going head-first into the powderhouse."

The minutes dragged. Twice Herndon swung the heavy hammer a few times, showering sparks and splintering wood so that the flames burned brighter. But the heavy iron hasps and the bolts that held them refused to yield.

The third time, the whole door fell open as the red-hot bolts burst through the charred pine. "Yeah, now!" they heard Herndon chortle. "Yeah, now."

He sloshed water on the fire and then used his hands to cup water and toss it on hot spots. No more smoke arose. No more steam arose. He pulled the half-burned door wide open and propped it back with the sledge hammer. He got down on his hands and knees and started to crawl into the powderhouse.

He had laid his .45 aside, and the Henry carbine leaned a few feet away, too far to do him any good in this vulnerable position, head-first down in the sunken powderhouse with his big hind end filling the doorway. Jim Pollock picked up a limber piece of green wood about four feet long and an inch thick.

He raced up the slope and swung the stick with both hands across Herndon's massive hindquarters. Herndon's bellow was muffled by the close quarters of the powderhouse, but it sounded as though his alarm was greater than his surprise.

"Grab hold," Jim shouted, "and pull the son-of-a-bitch out, everybody. Don't take no chances! If he fights back, brain him."

Herndon did not fight back. This was the end, and he knew it, and whatever guts he had ever possessed went out of him. They chained his arms behind him amd then brought the chain under his crotch and wound it around each leg. He was going to have to ride back down the slope on his belly, across his horse, but he would have two padlocks on him that took two different keys.

"Want to talk?" Hewitt asked him. "Or do you want to wait and tell it to the judge?"

"Mr. Hewitt," Herndon said, "I didn't hold up none of them places. Frank did."

Hewitt took note that he used the plural—not just one holdup, but several. "What do you expect, Herndon, a reward?" he asked.

"I found the money for you. Seems like that entitles me to part of the reward, if somebody will speak up to the judge for me."

"How about Charlotte, will she do?" said Hewitt. "You can put her on as a character witness—how about that?"

Herndon turned his face away and had nothing more to

say. Two of Jim Pollock's men got down in the powderhouse. First they handed out fifteen sticks of dynamite, and then a heavy leather pouch of Mexican manufacture. It had been made to close with a leather drawstring, but Frank Sanderson had used a small steel chain and another padlock.

"The hell with the chain," said Hewitt. "Just cut into the leather. We want plenty of witnesses as we count it, boys, so gather 'round."

There was $54,940 in the pouch, mostly in currency but some in gold coin. "Those pictures of them fellers you had took could turn out to be important, I reckon," Jim Pollock said. "Frank was doin' a pretty good business, looks like."

"We'll never get it all straightened out, Jim," said Hewitt. "He probably didn't steal all this money from the legal owners, but from the stick-up men instead."

"Who'll decide who gets it, the court?"

"If we let it go to court, the lawyers will end up with most of it. My partner and I are pretty good at working out compromises, and it's our case."

"I don't imagine you'll do it for free, though," Jim said.

"Not quite," said Hewitt. "As the Good Book says, the laborer is worthy of his hire."

Chapter Nineteen

"I hate to ask human beings to live in a place like this,"
Jim said. "I can fix it up snug and warm, but I don't see
why they can't stay in the house until I get a foreman's
house built."

"Jim, this will look like heaven to those two kids," said
Hewitt. "It'll be a home of their own, the first real home
either of them ever had."

"That girl will make it cozy," said Conrad. "She is a
nice girl. If dis is vat she vant, I vote to let her have it."

They were standing in the building Jim had had built a
few years ago for storing seed grain. Its inside dimensions
were fourteen by eighteen. The carpenter had put a
stovepipe hole through the roof and guyed a round, gal-
vanized chimney pipe above it. It served as a ventilator
for the seed, but it could also handle a big stove. And Jim
had a big, extra one.

"All right," said Jim, "I've got a couple of window
sashes I can put in myself, and I'll build them a partition
wherever they want it. But come spring, I'm going to
build them a nice little house."

It was rarely that Conrad Meuse left the office to come
out on a job with Hewitt, but there was enough potential
reward money in that $54,940 to make it pay. Besides,

Hewitt had to loaf somewhere until his arm healed, and Conrad had never seen Northern Arizona.

He had one more negotiating session day after tomorrow with five merchants who claimed the $14,940 that could not be considered part of the $40,000 NEAT loot. Actually they claimed a loss of $18,950, but Frank Sanderson had spent some of it on his mine and there was now not enough to go around.

Not one of them was Conrad's equal as a bargainer. He had only to threaten to throw it into the United States District Court, which was almost sure to award Bankers Bonding and Indemnity Company a 20 per cent fee for recovery. Hewitt had sat silent at the last meeting, letting Conrad handle it.

"We are willing to accept ten per cent," said Conrad.

"Oh sure, you're already walking off with better than fifteen thousand," someone said.

"Which my partner earned," said Conrad. "The opportunity was here. We will not discuss further the reward that you did not earn because Frank Sanderson had you terrified. Let us adjourn until after the wedding."

Tomorrow, Dick Easton and Charlotte Law—she refused to use Frank Sanderson's name—would be married in the Pollocks' parlor. Dick was already working as Jim's manager-foreman at $50 a month, plus housing. He would be given the use of a milk cow the year round. Charlie would take care of Edna's chickens and share in them and the eggs, and the two women would work the garden together.

Jim and Edna had started with less. Hewitt had told

Conrad, "I feel a strong personal interest in this girl and I'm going to make them a wedding gift of two hundred and fifty dollars, but I haven't got that much on me and I'm going to have to depend on you to supply me with an advance."

"Jeff," said Conrad, "you are a cheapskate, and this is a business expense. BB&I will pay five hundred. That is how we get a reputation for fair play and fair pay."

"I'm glad you brought that up. We're going to have to distribute a couple of thousand to the men who served on the posse and others who helped, including Jim's crew. When I'm out here on the job, I've got to have men at my back who know I've got a reputation for treating them fairly, and I'm glad you see it."

Conrad winced, but he said nothing. The New York owners had protested paying the $2,000 fee and expenses for Frank Sanderson, claiming there was no real proof that he had robbed the North East Arizona Transport stage. "Fine, ve meet you in court," said Conrad, his accent thickening as his temper shortened. "Ve haf list of sixty witnesses, and dis judge used to be director in a bank ve bond."

They agreed to pay but they still insisted that Hewitt's expense account of $1,912.87 was excessive, and for once Conrad took Hewitt's side. The 25 per cent reward for the recovery of the money—$10,000—was not a possible subject of argument.

If Conrad won his argument for 10 per cent of the unidentified money, the balance sheet on this job would look like this:

Reward for Frank Sanderson		$ 2,000.00
Expenses on Sanderson case		1,912.87
Recovery of money reward		10,000.00
10% of $14,940		1,494.00
Gross reward		$15,406.87
LESS:		
To Dick and Charlie	$ 500.00	
To members of posse	2,000.00	$ 2,500.00
Net reward		$12,906.87

"Do you know how long I have to work my tail off to make that much money?" Jim Pollock asked.

"I know from what I've seen that you could sell the Dot Four Dot for a hundred thousand dollars, easily," said Hewitt. "You haven't had many bad years."

"Yes," said Jim, "but I've never had any as good as that."

"You'd make a good field operative, and we can use one. We'll sell you a share of the business, a full one-third interest, for fifty thousand. We're turning down cases that I haven't got time to handle, and an old soldier like you could keep the money rolling in twelve months of the year. Of course, you wouldn't see much of Edna, but that's the life of a detective. That's why it's a job for a single man."

"Edna," Jim said, turning to his wife, "make him shut up. He's making that deal more and more tempting to me."

"Go ahead," she said. "I won't have any trouble getting someone to help me run the place."

Jim's hand closed over hers. Hewitt saw her squeeze back, and he felt the little pang that he suffered every now and then. He felt it again after the wedding the next day, when it came his turn to kiss the bride. Edna had defiantly dressed her all in white, even sending a rider to Prescott to bring back a dozen pairs of white shoes for her to try on.

There would always be a touch of sadness in this girl's memories, but it would fade a little each day. She was still in a healing process, and she needed lots of love, respect and just plain friendship.

She turned to him for his kiss. He cupped her face in his hands and said, "Charlie, you make that no-good Dick take care of you or I'll come back and nail his hide to the smokehouse door, and steal you myself."

He kissed her warm, yielding lips and knew what he was missing; but then he had always known that because he was a traveling man, not a marrying man. He did not release her face.

"Now," he said, "I want another little kiss for a wedding present I'm giving you. I'll give you a bill of sale for that mare, Sweetie, and you can raise a good horse from her every year until you and Dick start a spread of your own."

"Hey, you said you's gonna sell that horse back to me!" Jim Pollock squalled.

"Jim," said Hewitt, "you ought to know by now that you can't trust me."

I 27

"I'll tell you the kind of a day it was," Jim said that evening, when he and Hewitt and Conrad and Edna were eating supper in the kitchen and Dick and Charlie were eating in the unfinished shanty that was to be their temporary home.

"What kind of day is that?" Conrad asked.

"The kind that helps you forget that too many people call this Bloody Arizona," said Jim. "The kind that leads a man to hope that someday all of these riffraff gunnies will be wiped out, and it'll be safe to walk unarmed on any street in the Territory."

"But not yet," said Hewitt.

Jim shook his head sadly. "No, not yet."